Folktales of Japan

Collection of 38 Japanese folktales

Content

v

Green Willow

ITomodata, the young *samurai*, owed allegiance to the Lord of Noto. He was a soldier, a courtier, and a poet. He had a sweet voice and a beautiful face, a noble form and a very winning address. He was a graceful dancer, and excelled in every manly sport. He was wealthy and generous and kind. He was beloved by rich and by poor.

Now his *daimyo*, the Lord of Noto, wanted a man to undertake a mission of trust. He chose Tomodata, and called him to his presence.

"Are you loyal?" said the *daimyo*.

"My lord, you know it," answered Tomodata.

"Do you love me, then?" asked the *daimyo*.

"Ay, my good lord," said Tomodata, kneeling before him.

"Then carry my message," said the *daimyo*. "Ride and do not spare your beast. Ride straight, and fear not the mountains nor the enemies' country. Stay not for storm nor any other thing. Lose your life; but betray not your trust. Above all, do not look any maid between the eyes. Ride, and bring me word again quickly."

Thus spoke the Lord of Noto.

So Tomodata got him to horse, and away he rode upon his quest. Obedient to his lord's commands, he spared not his good beast. He rode straight, and was not afraid of the steep mountain passes nor of the enemies' country. Ere he had been three days upon the road the autumn tempest burst, for it was the ninth month. Down poured the rain in a torrent. Tomodata bowed his head and rode on. The wind howled in the pine- tree branches. It blew a typhoon. The good horse trembled and could scarcely keep its feet, but Tomodata spoke to it and urged it on. His own cloak he drew close about him and held it so that it might not blow away, and in this wise he rode on.

The fierce storm swept away many a familiar landmark of the road, and buffeted the *samurai* so that he became weary almost to fainting. Noontide was as dark as twilight, twilight was as dark as night, and when night fell it was as black as the night of Yomi, where lost souls wander and cry. By this time Tomodata had lost his way in a wild, lonely place, where, as it seemed to him, no human soul inhabited. His horse could carry him no longer, and he wandered on foot through bogs and marshes, through rocky and thorny tracks, until he fell into deep despair.

"Alack!" he cried, "must I die in this wilderness and the quest of the Lord of Noto be unfulfilled?"

At this moment the great winds blew away the clouds of the sky, so that the moon shone very brightly forth, and by the sudden light Tomodata saw a little hill on his right hand. Upon the hill was a small thatched cottage, and before the cottage grew three green weeping- willow trees.

"Now, indeed, the gods be thanked!" said Tomodata, and he climbed the hill in no time. Light shone from the chinks of the cottage door, and smoke curled out of a hole in the roof. The three willow trees swayed and flung out their green streamers in the wind. Tomodata threw his horse's rein over a branch of one of them, and called for admittance to the longed- for shelter.

At once the cottage door was opened by an old woman, very poorly but neatly clad.

"Who rides abroad upon such a night?" she asked, "and what wills he here?"

"I am a weary traveller, lost and benighted upon your lonely moor. My name is Tomodata. I am a *samurai* in the service of the Lord of Noto, upon whose business I ride. Show me hospitality for the love of the gods.

I crave food and shelter for myself and my horse."

As the young man stood speaking the water streamed from his garments. He reeled a little, and put out a hand to hold on by the side-post of the door.

"Come in, come in, young sir!" cried the old woman, full of pity. "Come in to the warm fire. You are very welcome. We have but coarse fare to offer, but it shall be set before you with great good- will. As to your horse, I see you have delivered him to my daughter; he is in good hands."

At this Tomodata turned sharply round. Just behind him, in the dim light, stood a very young girl with the horse's rein thrown over her arm. Her garments were blown about and her long loose hair streamed out upon the wind. The *samurai* wondered how she had come there. Then the old woman drew him into the cottage and shut the door. Before the fire sat the good man of the house, and the two old people did the very best they could for Tomodata. They gave him dry garments, comforted him with hot rice wine, and quickly prepared a good supper for him.

Presently the daughter of the house came in, and retired behind a screen to comb her hair and to dress afresh. Then she came forth to wait upon him. She wore a blue robe of homespun cotton. Her feet were bare. Her hair was not tied nor confined in any way, but lay along her smooth cheeks, and hung, straight and long and black, to her very knees. She was slender and graceful. Tomodata judged her to be about fifteen years old, and knew well that she was the fairest maiden he had ever seen.

At length she knelt at his side to pour wine into his cup. She held the wine- bottle in two hands and bent her head. Tomodata turned to look at her. When she had made an end of pouring the wine and had set down the bottle, their glances met, and Tomodata looked at her full between the eyes, for he forgot altogether the warning of his *daimyo*, the Lord of Noto.

"Maiden," he said, "what is your name?"

She answered: "They call me the Green Willow."

"The dearest name on earth," he said, and again he looked her between the eyes. And because he looked so long her face grew rosy red, from chin to forehead, and though she smiled her eyes filled with tears.

Ah me, for the Lord of Noto's quest!

Then Tomodata made this little song:

"*Long- haired maiden, do you know That with the red dawn I must go? Do you wish me far away? Cruel long- haired maiden, say- Long- haired maiden, if you know That with the red dawn I must go, Why, oh why, do you blush so?*"

And the maiden, the Green Willow, answered:

"*The dawn comes if I will or no; Never leave me, never go. My sleeve shall hide the blush away. The dawn comes if I will or no; Never leave me, never go. Lord, I lift my long sleeve so....*"

"Oh, Green Willow, Green Willow ..." sighed Tomodata.

That night he lay before the fire- still, but with wide eyes, for no sleep came to him though he was weary. He was sick for love of the Green Willow. Yet by the rules of his service he was bound in honour to think of no such thing. Moreover, he had the quest of the Lord of Noto that lay heavy on his heart, and he longed to keep truth and loyalty.

At the first peep of day he rose up. He looked upon the kind old man who had been his host, and left a purse of gold at his side as he slept. The maiden and her mother lay behind the screen.

Tomodata saddled and bridled his horse, and mounting, rode slowly away through the mist of the early morning. The storm was quite over and it was as still as Paradise. The green grass and the leaves shone with the wet. The sky was clear, and the path very bright with autumn flowers; but Tomodata was sad.

When the sunlight streamed across his saddlebow, "Ah, Green Willow, Green Willow," he sighed; and at noontide it was "Green Willow, Green Willow"; and "Green Willow, Green Willow," when the twilight fell. That night he lay in a deserted shrine, and the place was so holy that in spite of all he slept from midnight till the dawn. Then he rose, having it in his mind to wash himself in a cold stream that flowed near by, so as to go refreshed upon his journey; but he was stopped upon the shrine's threshold. There lay the Green Willow, prone upon the ground. A slender thing she lay, face downwards, with her black hair flung about her. She lifted a hand and held Tomodata by the sleeve. "My lord, my lord," she said, and fell to sobbing piteously.

He took her in his arms without a word, and soon he set her on his horse before him, and together they rode the livelong day. It was little they recked of the road they went, for all the while they looked into each other's eyes. The heat and the cold were nothing to them. They felt not the sun nor the rain; of truth or falsehood they thought nothing at all; nor of filial piety, nor of the Lord of Noto's quest, nor of honour nor plighted word. They knew but the one thing. Alas, for the ways of love!

At last they came to an unknown city, where they stayed. Tomodata carried gold and jewels in his girdle, so they found a house built of white wood, spread with sweet white mats. In every dim room there could be heard the sound of the garden waterfall, whilst the swallow flitted across and across the paper lattice. Here they dwelt, knowing but the one thing. Here they dwelt three years of happy days, and for Tomodata and the Green Willow the years were like garlands of sweet flowers.

In the autumn of the third year it chanced that the two of them went forth into the garden at dusk, for they had a wish to see the round moon rise; and as they watched, the Green Willow began to shake and shiver.

"My dear," said Tomodata, "you shake and shiver; and it is no wonder, the night wind is chill. Come in." And he put his arm around her.

At this she gave a long and pitiful cry, very loud and full of agony, and when she had uttered the cry she failed, and dropped her head upon her love's breast.

"Tomodata," she whispered, "say a prayer for me; I die."

"Oh, say not so, my sweet, my sweet! You are but weary; you are faint."

He carried her to the stream's side, where the iris grew like swords, and the lotus- leaves like shields, and laved her forehead with water. He said: "What is it, my dear? Look up and live."

"The tree," she moaned, "the tree... they have cut down my tree. Remember the Green Willow."

With that she slipped, as it seemed, from his arms to his feet; and he, casting himself upon the ground, found only silken garments, bright coloured, warm and sweet, and straw sandals, scarlet- thonged.

In after years, when Tomodata was a holy man, he travelled from shrine to shrine, painfully upon his feet, and acquired much merit.

Once, at nightfall, he found himself upon a lonely moor. On his right hand he beheld a little hill, and on it the sad ruins of a poor thatched cottage. The door swung to and fro with broken latch and creaking hinge. Before it stood three old stumps of willow trees that had long since been cut down. Tomodata stood for a long time still and silent. Then he sang gently to himself:

"*Long- haired maiden, do you know That with the red dawn I must go? Do you wish me far away? Cruel long- haired maiden, say- Long- haired maiden, if you know That with the red dawn I must go, Why, oh why, do you blush so?*"

"Ah, foolish song! The gods forgive me.... I should have recited the Holy Sutra for the Dead," said Tomodata.

The Flute

Long since, there lived in Yed(
of good lineage and very honest
His wife was a gentle and loving lady. To his
secret grief, she bore him no sons. But a
daughter she did give him, whom they called
O'Yoné, which, being interpreted, is "Rice in
the ear." Each of them loved this child more
than life, and guarded her as the apple of their
eye. And the child grew up red and white, and
long- eyed, straight and slender as the green
bamboo.

When O'Yoné was twelve years old, her
mother drooped with the fall of the year,
sickened, and pined, and ere the red had faded
from the leaves of the maples she was dead
and shrouded and laid in the earth. The
husband was wild in his grief. He cried aloud,
he beat his breast, he lay upon the ground and
refused comfort, and for days he neither
broke his fast nor slept. The child was quite
silent.

Time passed by. The man perforce went
about his business. The snows of winter fell
and covered his wife's grave. The beaten
pathway from his house to the dwelling of the
dead was snow also, undisturbed save for the
faint prints of a child's sandalled feet. In the

...ng- time he girded up his robe and went ...orth to see the cherry blossom, making merry enough, and writing a poem upon gilded paper, which he hung to a cherry- tree branch to flutter in the wind. The poem was in praise of the spring and of *sake*. Later, he planted the orange lily of forgetfulness, and thought of his wife no more. But the child remembered.

Before the year was out he brought a new bride home, a woman with a fair face and a black heart. But the man, poor fool, was happy, and commended his child to her, and believed that all was well.

Now because her father loved O'Yoné, her stepmother hated her with a jealous and deadly hatred, and every day she dealt cruelly by the child, whose gentle ways and patience only angered her the more. But because of her father's presence she did not dare to do O'Yoné any great ill; therefore she waited, biding her time. The poor child passed her days and her nights in torment and horrible fear. But of these things she said not a word to her father. Such is the manner of children.

Now, after some time, it chanced that the man was called away by his business to a distant city. Kioto was the name of the city, and from Yedo it is many days' journey on foot or on horseback. Howbeit, go the man needs must, and stay there three moons or more. Therefore he made ready, and equipped himself, and his servants that were to go with him, with all things needful; and so came to the last night before his departure, which was to be very early in the morning.

He called O'Yoné to him and said: "Come here, then, my dear little daughter." So O'Yoné went and knelt before him.

"What gift shall I bring you home from Kioto?" he said.

But she hung her head and did not answer.

"Answer, then, rude little one," he bade her. "Shall it be a golden fan, or a roll of silk, or a new *obi* of red brocade, or a great battledore with images upon it and many light- feathered shuttlecocks?"

Then she burst into bitter weeping, and he took her upon his knees to soothe her. But she hid her face with her sleeves and cried as if her heart would break. And, "O father, father, father," she said, "do not go away- do not go away!"

"But, my sweet, I needs must," he answered, "and soon I shall be back- so soon, scarcely it will seem that I am gone, when I shall be here again with fair gifts in my hand."

"Father, take me with you," she said.

"Alas, what a great way for a little girl! Will you walk on your feet, my little pilgrim, or mount a pack- horse? And how would you fare in the inns of Kioto? Nay, my dear, stay; it is but for a little time, and your kind mother will be with you."

She shuddered in his arms.

"Father, if you go, you will never see me more."

Then the father felt a sudden chill about his heart, that gave him pause. But he would not heed it. What! Must he, a strong man grown, be swayed by a child's fancies? He put O'Yoné gently from him, and she slipped away as silently as a shadow.

But in the morning she came to him before sunrise with a little flute in her hand, fashioned of bamboo and smoothly polished. "I made it myself," she said, "from a bamboo in the grove that is behind our garden. I made it for you. As you cannot take me with you, take the little flute, honourable father. Play on it sometimes, if you will, and think of me." Then she wrapped it in a handkerchief of white silk, lined with scarlet, and wound a scarlet cord about it, and gave it to her father, who put it in his sleeve. After this he departed and went his way, taking the road to Kioto. As he went he looked back thrice, and beheld his child, standing at the gate, looking after him. Then the road turned and he saw her no more.

The city of Kioto was passing great and beautiful, and so the father of O'Yoné found it. And what with his business during the day, which sped very well, and his pleasure in the evening, and his sound sleep at night, the time passed merrily, and small thought he gave to Yedo, to his home, or to his child. Two moons passed, and three, and he made no plans for return.

One evening he was making ready to go forth to a great supper of his friends, and as he searched in his chest for certain brave silken *hakama* which he intended to wear as an honour to the feast, he came upon the little flute, which had lain hidden all this time in the sleeve of his travelling dress. He drew it forth from its red and white handkerchief, and as he did so, felt strangely cold with an icy chill that crept about his heart. He hung over the live charcoal of the *hibachi* as one in a dream. He put the flute to his lips, when there came from it a long- drawn wail.

He dropped it hastily upon the mats and clapped his hands for his servant, and told him he would not go forth that night. He was not well, he would be alone. After a long time he reached out his hand for the flute. Again that long, melancholy cry. He shook from head to foot, but he blew into the flute. "Come back to Yedo... come back to Yedo.... Father! Father!" The quavering childish voice rose to a shriek and then broke.

A horrible foreboding now took possession of the man, and he was as one beside himself. He flung himself from the house and from the city, and journeyed day and night, denying himself sleep and food. So pale was he and wild that the people deemed him a madman and fled from him, or pitied him as the afflicted of the gods. At last he came to his journey's end, travel- stained from head to heel, with bleeding feet and half- dead of weariness.

His wife met him in the gate.

He said: "Where is the child?"

"The child...?" she answered.

"Ay, the child- my child... where is she?" he cried in an agony.

The woman laughed: "Nay, my lord, how should I know? She is within at her books, or she is in the garden, or she is asleep, or mayhap she has gone forth with her playmates, or ..."

He said: "Enough; no more of this. Come, where is my child?"

Then she was afraid. And, "In the Bamboo Grove," she said, looking at him with wide eyes.

There the man ran, and sought O'Yoné among the green stems of the bamboos. But he did not find her. He called, "Yoné! Yoné!" and again, "Yoné! Yoné!" But he had no answer; only the wind sighed in the dry bamboo leaves. Then he felt in his sleeve and brought forth the little flute, and very tenderly put it to his lips. There was a faint sighing sound. Then a voice spoke, thin and pitiful:

"Father, dear father, my wicked stepmother killed me. Three moons since she killed me. She buried me in the clearing of the Bamboo Grove. You may find my bones. As for me, you will never see me any more- you will never see me more...."

With his own two- handed sword the man did justice, and slew his wicked wife, avenging the death of his innocent child. Then he dressed himself in coarse white raiment, with a great rice- straw hat that shadowed his face. And he took a staff and a straw rain- coat and bound sandals on his feet, and thus he set forth upon a pilgrimage to the holy places of Japan.

And he carried the little flute with him, in a fold of his garment, upon his breast.

The Tea- Kettle

Long ago, as I've heard tell, there dwelt at the temple of Morinji, in the Province of Kotsuke, a holy priest.

Now there were three things about this reverend man. First, he was wrapped up in meditations and observances and forms and doctrines. He was a great one for the Sacred Sutras, and knew strange and mystical things. Then he had a fine exquisite taste of his own, and nothing pleased him so much as the ancient tea ceremony of the *Cha- no- yu*; and for the third thing about him, he knew both sides of a copper coin well enough and loved a bargain.

None so pleased as he when he happened upon an ancient tea- kettle, lying rusty and dirty and half- forgotten in a corner of a poor shop in a back street of his town.

"An ugly bit of old metal," says the holy man to the shopkeeper; "but it will do well enough to boil my humble drop of water of an evening. I'll give you three *rin* for it." This he did and took the kettle home, rejoicing; for it was of bronze, fine work, the very thing for the *Cha- no- yu.*

A novice cleaned and scoured the tea- kettle, and it came out as pretty as you please.

The priest turned it this way and that, and upside down, looked into it, tapped it with his finger- nail. He smiled. "A bargain," he cried, "a bargain!" and rubbed his hands. He set the kettle upon a box covered over with a purple cloth, and looked at it so long that first he was fain to rub his eyes many times, and then to close them altogether. His head dropped forward and he slept.

And then, believe me, the wonderful thing happened. The tea- kettle moved, though no hand was near it. A hairy head, with two bright eyes, looked out of the spout. The lid jumped up and down. Four brown and hairy paws appeared, and a fine bushy tail. In a minute the kettle was down from the box and going round and round looking at things.

"A very comfortable room, to be sure," says the tea- kettle.

Pleased enough to find itself so well lodged, it soon began to dance and to caper nimbly and to sing at the top of its voice. Three or four novices were studying in the next room. "The old man is lively," they said; "only hark to him. What can he be at?" And they laughed in their sleeves.

Heaven's mercy, the noise that the tea- kettle made! Bang! bang! Thud! thud! thud!

The novices soon stopped laughing. One of them slid aside the *kara-kami* and peeped through.

"Arah, the devil and all's in it!" he cried. "Here's the master's old tea-kettle turned into a sort of a badger. The gods protect us from witchcraft, or for certain we shall be lost!"

"And I scoured it not an hour since," said another novice, and he fell to reciting the Holy Sutras on his knees.

A third laughed. "I'm for a nearer view of the hobgoblin," he said.

So the lot of them left their books in a twinkling, and gave chase to the tea-kettle to catch it. But could they come up with the tea-kettle? Not a bit of it. It danced and it leapt and it flew up into the air. The novices rushed here and there, slipping upon the mats. They grew hot. They grew breathless.

"Ha, ha! Ha, ha!" laughed the tea-kettle; and "Catch me if you can!" laughed the wonderful tea-kettle.

Presently the priest awoke, all rosy, the holy man.

"And what's the meaning of this racket," he says, "disturbing me at my holy meditations and all?"

"Master, master," cry the novices, panting and mopping their brows, "your tea-kettle is bewitched. It was a badger, no less. And the dance it has been giving us, you'd never believe!"

"Stuff and nonsense," says the priest; "bewitched? Not a bit of it. There it rests on its box, good quiet thing, just where I put it."

Sure enough, so it did, looking as hard and cold and innocent as you please. There was not a hair of a badger near it. It was the novices that looked foolish.

"A likely story indeed," says the priest. "I have heard of the pestle that took wings to itself and flew away, parting company with the mortar. That is easily to be understood by any man. But a kettle that turned into a badger-no, no! To your books, my sons, and pray to be preserved from the perils of illusion."

That very night the holy man filled the kettle with water from the spring and set it on the *hibachi* to boil for his cup of tea. When the water began to boil-

"Ai! Ai!" the kettle cried; "Ai! Ai! The heat of the Great Hell!" And it lost no time at all, but hopped off the fire as quick as you please.

"Sorcery!" cried the priest. "Black magic! A devil! A devil! A devil! Mercy on me! Help! Help! Help!" He was frightened out of his wits, the dear good man. All the novices came running to see what was the matter.

"The tea- kettle is bewitched," he gasped; "it was a badger, assuredly it was a badger... it both speaks and leaps about the room."

"Nay, master," said a novice, "see where it rests upon its box, good quiet thing."

And sure enough, so it did.

"Most reverend sir," said the novice, "let us all pray to be preserved from the perils of illusion."

The priest sold the tea- kettle to a tinker and got for it twenty copper coins.

"It's a mighty fine bit of bronze," says the priest. "Mind, I'm giving it away to you, I'm sure I cannot tell what for." Ah, he was the one for a bargain! The tinker was a happy man and carried home the kettle. He turned it this way and that, and upside down, and looked into it.

"A pretty piece," says the tinker; "a very good bargain." And when he went to bed that night he put the kettle by him, to see it first thing in the morning.

He awoke at midnight and fell to looking at the kettle by the bright light of the moon.

Presently it moved, though there was no hand near it.

"Strange," said the tinker; but he was a man who took things as they came.

A hairy head, with two bright eyes, looked out of the kettle's spout. The lid jumped up and down. Four brown and hairy paws appeared, and a fine bushy tail. It came quite close to the tinker and laid a paw upon him.

"Well?" says the tinker.

"I am not wicked," says the tea-kettle.

"No," says the tinker.

"But I like to be well treated. I am a badger tea-kettle."

"So it seems," says the tinker.

"At the temple they called me names, and beat me and set me on the fire. I couldn't stand it, you know."

"I like your spirit," says the tinker.

"I think I shall settle down with you."

"Shall I keep you in a lacquer box?" says the tinker.

"Not a bit of it, keep me with you; let us have a talk now and again. I am very fond of a pipe. I like rice to eat, and beans and sweet things."

"A cup of *saké* sometimes?" says the tinker.

"Well, yes, now you mention it."

"I'm willing," says the tinker.

"Thank you kindly," says the tea-kettle; "and, as a beginning, would you object to my sharing your bed? The night has turned a little chilly."

"Not the least in the world," says the tinker.

The tinker and the tea- kettle became the best of friends. They ate and talked together. The kettle knew a thing or two and was very good company.

One day: "Are you poor?" says the kettle.

"Yes," says the tinker, "middling poor."

"Well, I have a happy thought. For a tea-kettle, I am out- of- the- way- really very accomplished."

"I believe you," says the tinker.

"My name is *Bumbuku- Chagama*; I am the very prince of Badger Tea- Kettles."

"Your servant, my lord," says the tinker.

"If you'll take my advice," says the tea-kettle, "you'll carry me round as a show; I really am out- of- the- way, and it's my opinion you'd make a mint of money."

"That would be hard work for you, my dear *Bumbuku*," says the tinker.

"Not at all; let us start forthwith," says the tea- kettle.

So they did. The tinker bought hangings for a theatre, and he called the show *Bumbuku-Chagama*. How the people flocked to see the fun! For the wonderful and most accomplished tea- kettle danced and sang, and walked the tight rope as to the manner born. It played such tricks and had such droll ways that the people laughed till their sides ached. It was a treat to see the tea- kettle bow as gracefully as a lord and thank the people for their patience.

The *Bumbuku- Chagama* was the talk of the country- side, and all the gentry came to see it as well as the commonalty. As for the tinker, he waved a fan and took the money. You may believe that he grew fat and rich. He even went to Court, where the great ladies and the royal princesses made much of the wonderful tea- kettle.

At last the tinker retired from business, and to him the tea- kettle came with tears in its bright eyes.

"I'm much afraid it's time to leave you," it says.

"Now, don't say that, *Bumbuku*, dear," says the tinker. "We'll be so happy together now we are rich."

"I've come to the end of my time," says the tea- kettle. "You'll not see old *Bumbuku* any more; henceforth I shall be an ordinary kettle, nothing more or less."

"Oh, my dear *Bumbuku*, what shall I do?" cried the poor tinker in tears.

"I think I should like to be given to the temple of Morinji, as a very sacred treasure," says the tea- kettle.

It never spoke or moved again. So the tinker presented it as a very sacred treasure to the temple, and the half of his wealth with it.

And the tea- kettle was held in wondrous fame for many a long year. Some persons even worshipped it as a saint.

The Peony Lantern

In Yedo there dwelt a *samurai* called Hagiwara. He was a *samurai* of the *hatamoto*, which is of all the ranks of *samurai* the most honourable. He possessed a noble figure and a very beautiful face, and was beloved of many a lady of Yedo, both openly and in secret. For himself, being yet very young, his thoughts turned to pleasure rather than to love, and morning, noon and night he was wont to disport himself with the gay youth of the city. He was the prince and leader of joyous revels within doors and without, and would often parade the streets for long together with bands of his boon companions.

One bright and wintry day during the Festival of the New Year he found himself with a company of laughing youths and maidens playing at battledore and shuttlecock. He had wandered far away from his own quarter of the city, and was now in a suburb quite the other side of Yedo, where the streets were empty, more or less, and the quiet houses stood in gardens. Hagiwara wielded his heavy battledore with great skill and grace, catching the gilded shuttlecock and tossing it lightly into the air; but at length with a careless or an ill- judged stroke, he sent it flying over the heads of the players, and over the bamboo fence of a garden near by. Immediately he started after it. Then his companions cried, "Stay, Hagiwara; here we have more than a dozen shuttlecocks."

"Nay," he said, "but this was dove-coloured and gilded."

"Foolish one!" answered his friends; "here we have six shuttlecocks all dove- coloured and gilded."

But he paid them no heed, for he had become full of a very strange desire for the shuttlecock he had lost. He scaled the bamboo fence and dropped into the garden which was upon the farther side. Now he had marked the very spot where the shuttlecock should have fallen, but it was not there; so he searched along the foot of the bamboo fence—but no, he could not find it. Up and down he went, beating the bushes with his battledore, his eyes on the ground, drawing breath heavily as if he had lost his dearest treasure. His friends called him, but he did not come, and they grew tired and went to their own homes. The light of day began to fail. Hagiwara, the *samurai*, looked up and saw a girl standing a few yards away from him. She beckoned him with her right hand, and in her left she

35

held a gilded shuttlecock with dove- coloured feathers.

The *samurai* shouted joyfully and ran forward. Then the girl drew away from him, still beckoning him with the right hand. The shuttlecock lured him, and he followed. So they went, the two of them, till they came to the house that was in the garden, and three stone steps that led up to it. Beside the lowest step there grew a plum tree in blossom, and upon the highest step there stood a fair and very young lady. She was most splendidly attired in robes of high festival. Her *kimono* was of water- blue silk, with sleeves of ceremony so long that they touched the ground; her under- dress was scarlet, and her great girdle of brocade was stiff and heavy with gold. In her hair were pins of gold and tortoiseshell and coral.

When Hagiwara saw the lady, he knelt down forthwith and made her due obeisance, till his forehead touched the ground.

Then the lady spoke, smiling with pleasure like a child. "Come into my house, Hagiwara Sama, *samurai* of the *hatamoto*. I am O'Tsuyu, the Lady of the Morning Dew. My dear handmaiden, O'Yoné, has brought you to me. Come in, Hagiwara Sama, *samurai* of the *hatamoto*; for indeed I am glad to see you, and happy is this hour."

So the *samurai* went in, and they brought him to a room of ten mats, where they entertained him; for the Lady of the Morning Dew danced before him in the ancient manner, whilst O'Yoné, the handmaiden, beat upon a small scarlet- tasselled drum.

Afterwards they set food before him, the red rice of the festival and sweet warm wine, and he ate and drank of the food they gave him.

It was dark night when Hagiwara took his leave. "Come again, honourable lord, come again," said O'Yoné the handmaiden.

"Yea, lord, you needs must come," whispered the Lady of the Morning Dew.

The *samurai* laughed. "And if I do not come?" he said mockingly. "What if I do not come?"

The lady stiffened, and her child's face grew grey, but she laid her hand upon Hagiwara's shoulder.

"Then," she said, "it will be death, lord. Death it will be for you and for me. There is no other way." O'Yoné shuddered and hid her eyes with her sleeve.

The *samurai* went out into the night, being very much afraid.

Long, long he sought for his home and could not find it, wandering in the black darkness from end to end of the sleeping city. When at last he reached his familiar door the late dawn was almost come, and wearily he threw himself upon his bed. Then he laughed. "After all, I have left behind me my shuttlecock," said Hagiwara the *samurai*.

The next day Hagiwara sat alone in his house from morning till evening. He had his hands before him; and he thought, but did nothing more. At the end of the time he said, "It is a joke that a couple of *geisha* have sought to play on me. Excellent, in faith, but they shall not have me!" So he dressed himself in his best and went forth to join his friends. For five or six days he was at joustings and junketings, the gayest of the gay. His wit was ready, his spirits were wild.

Then he said, "By the gods, I am deathly sick of this," and took to walking the streets of Yedo alone. From end to end of the great city he went. He wandered by day and he wandered by night, by street and alley he went, by hill and moat and castle wall, but he found not what he sought. He could not come upon the garden where his shuttlecock was lost, nor yet upon the Lady of the Morning Dew. His spirit had no rest. He fell sick and took to his bed, where he neither ate nor slept, but grew spectre- thin. This was about the third month. In the sixth month, at the time of *niubai*, the hot and rainy season, he rose up, and, in spite of all his faithful servant could say or do to dissuade him, he wrapped a loose summer robe about him and at once went forth.

"Alack! Alack!" cried the servant, "the youth has the fever, or he is perchance mad."

Hagiwara faltered not at all. He looked neither to the right nor to the left. Straight forward he went, for he said to himself, "All roads lead past my love's house." Soon he came to a quiet suburb, and to a certain house whose garden had a split bamboo fence. Hagiwara laughed softly and scaled the fence.

"The same, the very same shall be the manner of our meeting," he said. He found the garden wild and overgrown. Moss covered the three stone steps. The plum tree that grew there fluttered its green leaves disconsolate. The house was still, its shutters were all closed, it was forlorn and deserted.

The *samurai* grew cold as he stood and wondered. A soaking rain fell.

There came an old man into the garden. He said to Hagiwara:

"Sir, what do you do here?"

"The white flower has fallen from the plum tree," said the *samurai*. "Where is the Lady of the Morning Dew?"

"She is dead," answered the old man; "dead these five or six moons, of a strange and sudden sickness. She lies in the graveyard on the hill, and O'Yoné, her handmaid, lies by her side. She could not suffer her mistress to wander alone through the long night of Yomi. For their sweet spirits' sake I would still tend this garden, but I am old and it is little that I can do. Oh, sir, they are dead indeed. The grass grows on their graves."

Hagiwara went to his own home. He took a slip of pure white wood and he wrote upon it, in large fair characters, the dear name of his lady. This he set up, and burned before it incense and sweet odours, and made every offering that was meet, and did due observance, and all for the welfare of her departed spirit.

Then drew near the Festival of *Bon*, the time of returning souls. The good folk of Yedo took lanterns and visited their graves. Bringing food and flowers, they cared for their beloved dead. On the thirteenth day of the seventh month, which, in the *Bon*, is the day of days, Hagiwara the *samurai* walked in his garden by night for the sake of the coolness. It was windless and dark. A cicala hidden in the heart of a pomegranate flower sang shrilly now and again. Now and again a carp leaped in the round pond. For the rest it was still, and never a leaf stirred.

About the hour of the Ox, Hagiwara heard the sound of footsteps in the lane that lay beyond his garden hedge. Nearer and nearer they came.

"Women's *geta*," said the *samurai*. He knew them by the hollow echoing noise. Looking over his rose hedge, he saw two slender women come out of the dimness hand in hand. One of them carried a lantern with a bunch of peony flowers tied to the handle. It was such a lantern as is used at the time of the *Bon* in the service of the dead. It swung as the two women walked, casting an uncertain light. As they came abreast of the *samurai* upon the other side of the hedge, they turned their faces to him. He knew them at once, and gave one great cry.

The girl with the peony lantern held it up so that the light fell upon him.

"Hagiwara Sama," she cried, "by all that is most wonderful! Why, lord, we were told that you were dead. We have daily recited the *Nembutsu* for your soul these many moons!"

41

"Come in, come in, O'Yoné," he said; "and is it indeed your mistress that you hold by the hand? Can it be my lady?... Oh, my love!"

O'Yoné answered, "Who else should it be?" and the two came in at the garden gate.

But the Lady of the Morning Dew held up her sleeve to hide her face.

"How was it I lost you?" said the *samurai*; "how was it I lost you, O'Yoné?"

"Lord," she said, "we have moved to a little house, a very little house, in the quarter of the city which is called the Green Hill. We were suffered to take nothing with us there, and we are grown very poor. With grief and want my mistress is become pale."

Then Hagiwara took his lady's sleeve to draw it gently from her face.

"Lord," she sobbed, "you will not love me, I am not fair."

But when he looked upon her his love flamed up within him like a consuming fire, and shook him from head to foot. He said never a word.

She drooped. "Lord," she murmured, "shall I go or stay?"

And he said, "Stay."

A little before daybreak the *samurai* fell into a deep sleep, and awoke to find himself alone in the clear light of the morning. He lost not an instant, but rose and went forth, and immediately made his way through Yedo to the quarter of the city which is called the Green Hill. Here he inquired for the house of the Lady of the Morning Dew, but no one could direct him. High and low he searched fruitlessly. It seemed to him that for the second time he had lost his dear lady, and he turned homewards in bitter despair. His way led him through the grounds of a certain temple, and as he went he marked two graves that were side by side. One was little and obscure, but the other was marked by a fair monument, like the tomb of some great one. Before the monument there hung a lantern with a bunch of peony flowers tied to its handle. It was such a lantern as is used at the time of *Bon* in the service of the dead.

Long, long did the *samurai* stand as one in a dream. Then he smiled a little and said:

"'*We have moved to a little house... a very little house... upon the Green Hill... we were suffered to take nothing with us there and we are grown very poor... with grief and want my mistress is become pale....*' A little house, a dark house, yet you will make room for me, oh, my beloved, pale one of my desires. We have loved for the space of ten existences, leave me not now... my dear." Then he went home.

His faithful servant met him and cried:

"Now what ails you, master?"

He said, "Why, nothing at all.... I was never merrier."

But the servant departed weeping, and saying, "The mark of death is on his face... and I, whither shall I go that bore him as a child in these arms?"

Every night, for seven nights, the maidens with the peony lantern came to Hagiwara's dwelling. Fair weather or foul was the same to them. They came at the hour of the Ox. There was mystic wooing. By the strong bond of illusion the living and the dead were bound together.

On the seventh night the servant of the *samurai*, wakeful with fear and sorrow, made bold to peer into his lord's room through a crack in the wooden shutters. His hair stood on end and his blood ran cold to see Hagiwara in the arms of a fearful thing, smiling up at the horror that was its face, stroking its dank green robe with languid fingers. With daylight the servant made his way to a holy man of his acquaintance. When he had told his tale he asked, "Is there any hope for Hagiwara Sama?"

"Alack," said the holy man, "who can withstand the power of Karma? Nevertheless, there is a little hope." So he told the servant what he must do. Before nightfall, this one had set a sacred text above every door and window- place of his master's house, and he had rolled in the silk of his master's girdle a golden emblem of the Tathagata. When these things were done, Hagiwara being drawn two ways became himself as weak as water. And his servant took him in his arms, laid him upon his bed and covered him lightly, and saw him fall into a deep sleep.

At the hour of the Ox there was heard the sound of footsteps in the lane, without the garden hedge. Nearer and nearer they came. They grew slow and stopped.

"What means this, O'Yoné, O'Yoné?" said a piteous voice. "The house is asleep, and I do not see my lord."

"Come home, sweet lady, Hagiwara's heart is changed."

"That I will not, O'Yoné, O'Yoné... you must find a way to bring me to my lord."

"Lady, we cannot enter here. See the Holy Writing over every door and window- place... we may not enter here."

There was a sound of bitter weeping and a long wail.

"Lord, I have loved thee through the space of ten existences." Then the footsteps retreated and their echo died away.

The next night it was quite the same. Hagiwara slept in his weakness; his servant watched; the wraiths came and departed in sobbing despair.

The third day, when Hagiwara went to the bath, a thief stole the emblem, the golden emblem of the Tathagata, from his girdle. Hagiwara did not mark it. But that night he lay awake. It was his servant that slept, worn out with watching. Presently a great rain fell and Hagiwara, waking, heard the sound of it upon the roof. The heavens were opened and for hours the rain fell. And it tore the holy text from over the round window in Hagiwara's chamber.

At the hour of the Ox there was heard the sound of footsteps in the lane without the garden hedge. Nearer and nearer they came. They grew slow and stopped.

"This is the last time, O'Yoné, O'Yoné, therefore bring me to my lord. Think of the love of ten existences. Great is the power of Karma. There must be a way...."

"Come, my beloved," called Hagiwara with a great voice.

"Open, lord... open and I come."

But Hagiwara could not move from his couch.

"Come, my beloved," he called for the second time.

"I cannot come, though the separation wounds me like a sharp sword. Thus we suffer for the sins of a former life." So the lady spoke and moaned like the lost soul that she was. But O'Yoné took her hand.

"See the round window," she said.

Hand in hand the two rose lightly from the earth. Like vapour they passed through the unguarded window. The *samurai* called, "Come to me, beloved," for the third time.

He was answered, "Lord, I come."

In the grey morning Hagiwara's servant found his master cold and dead. At his feet stood the peony lantern burning with a weird yellow flame. The servant shivered, took up the lantern and blew out the light; for "I cannot bear it," he said.

The Sea King and the Magic Jewels

This is a tale beloved by the children of Japan, and by the old folk- a tale of magical jewels and a visit to the Sea King's palace.

Prince Rice- Ear- Ruddy- Plenty loved a beautiful and royal maiden, and made her his bride. And the lady was called Princess Blossoming- Brightly- as- the- Flowers- of- the- Trees, so sweetly fair was she. But her father was augustly wrath at her betrothal, for his Augustness, Prince Rice- Ear- Ruddy- Plenty, had put aside her elder sister, the Princess of the Rocks (and, indeed, this lady was not fair), for he loved only Princess Blossoming- Brightly. So the old King said, "Because of this, the offspring of these heavenly deities shall be frail, fading and falling like the flowers of the trees." So it is. At this day, the lives of their Augustnesses, the Heavenly Sovereigns, are not long.

Howbeit, in the fullness of time, the lady, Blossoming- Brightly- as- the- Flowers- of- the- Trees, bore two lovely men children, and called the elder Fire Flash and the younger Fire Fade.

Prince Fire Flash was a fisherman, who got his luck upon the wide sea, and ran upon the shore with his august garments girded. And again, he tarried all the night in his boat, upon the high wave- crests. And he caught things broad of fin and things narrow of fin, and he was a deity of the water weeds and of the waters and of the fishes of the sea.

But Prince Fire Fade was a hunter, who got his luck upon the mountains and in the forest, who bound sandals fast upon his feet, and bore a bow and heavenly- feathered arrows. And he caught things rough of hair and things soft of hair, and he knew the trail of the badger and the wild cherry's time of flowering. For he was a deity of the woods.

Now Prince Fire Fade spoke to his elder brother, Prince Fire Flash, and said, "Brother, I am aweary of the green hills. Therefore let us now exchange our luck. Give me thy rod and I will go to the cool waters. Thou mayest take my great bow and all my heavenly-feathered arrows and try the mountains, where, trust me, thou shalt see many strange and beautiful things, unknown to thee before."

But Prince Fire Flash answered, "Not so... not so."

And again, after not many days were past, Prince Fire Fade came and sighed, "I am aweary of the green hills... the fair waters call me. Woe to be a younger brother!" And when

Prince Fire Flash took no heed of him, but angled with his rod, day and night, and caught things broad of fin and things narrow of fin, Prince Fire Fade drooped with desire, and let his long hair fall untended upon his shoulders. And he murmured, "Oh, to try my luck upon the sea!" till at last Prince Fire Flash, his elder brother, gave him the rod for very weariness, and betook himself to the mountains. And all day he hunted, and let fly the heavenly-feathered arrows; but rough of hair or soft of hair, never a thing did he catch. And he cried, "Fool, fool, to barter the heavenly luck of the gods!" So he returned.

And his Augustness, Prince Fire Fade, took the luck of the sea, and angled in sunshine and in gloom; but broad of fin or narrow of fin, never a fish did he catch. And, moreover, he lost his brother's fish- hook in the sea. So he hung his head, and returned.

And Prince Fire Flash said, "Each to his own, the hunter to the mountain, and the fisherman to the sea... for thou and I have brought nothing home, and this night we sleep hungry. We may not barter the luck of the gods. And now, where is my fish- hook?"

So Prince Fire Fade replied, saying softly, "Sweet brother, be not angry... but, toiling all day with thy fish- hook, broad of fin or narrow of fin, not a fish did I catch; and, at the last, I lost thy fish- hook in the sea."

At this his Highness, Prince Fire Flash, flew into a great rage, and stamping his feet, required the fish- hook of his brother.

And Prince Fire Fade made answer, "Sweet brother, I have not thy fish- hook, but the deep sea, whose bottom no man may search. Though I should die for thee, yet could I not give thee back thy fish- hook."

But his elder brother required it of him the more urgently.

Then Prince Fire Fade burst the wild wistaria tendrils which bound his august ten-grasp sword to his side. And he said, "Farewell, good sword." And he broke it into many fragments, and made five hundred fish-hooks to give to his brother, Prince Fire Flash. But Prince Fire Flash would have none of them.

And again Prince Fire Fade toiled at a great furnace, and made one thousand fish- hooks; and upon his knees he humbly offered them to his brother, Prince Fire Flash. For he loved his brother. Nevertheless Prince Fire Flash would not so much as look at them, but sat moody, his head on his hand, saying, "Mine own lost fish- hook will I have, that and no other."

So Prince Fire Fade went grieving from the palace gates, and wandered lamenting by the seashore; and his tears fell and mingled with the foam. And, when night came, he had no heart to return homewards, but sat down, weary, upon a rock amid the salt pools. And he cried, "Alas, my brother, I am all to blame, and through my foolishness has this come upon me. But oh, my brother, together were we nursed upon the sweet breast of our mother, Princess Blossoming- Brightly- as- the- Flowers- of- the- Trees, for almost hand in hand did we come into the world."

And the moon rose so that the sea and the Central Land of Reed Plains was light. But Prince Fire Fade ceased not to lament.

Then Shiko- Tsuchi- no- Kami, the Lord of Sea Salt, came with the rising tide, and spoke, "Wherefore weeps the Heaven's Sky Height?"

And Prince Fire Fade made answer: "I have taken my brother's fish- hook, and I have lost it in the sea. And though I have given him many other fish- hooks for compensation, he will have none of them, but desires only the original fish- hook. Truly, the gods know, I would give my life to find it; but how should that serve?"

And Shiko- Tsuchi- no- Kami took him by the sleeve to where a boat moved upon the water, and set him in the boat and pushed it from the shore, saying, "My son, pursue the pleasant path that Tsuki- Yomi- no- Kami, His Augustness, the Moon Night Possessor, has made for thee upon the waters. And, at the end, thou shalt come to a palace made of fishes' scales, which is the palace of the great King of the Sea. Before the gate there is a clear well, and by the well- side there grows a cassia tree with many spreading branches. Therefore climb thou into the branches of the cassia tree, and there wait for the King's daughter, who shall come to give thee counsel."

And Prince Fire Fade, standing up in the boat, made obeisance, and thanked the Lord of Sea Salt. But this one girded his august garments and pushed the boat before him, till he was thigh- deep in the water. And he said, "Nay, nay, fair youth, no thanks, only do my bidding."

So his Augustness, Prince Fire Fade, came to the Sea King's palace. And he forthwith climbed the cassia tree and waited among its green branches.

At the day's dawning came the handmaidens of the Sea King's daughter, with their jewelled vessels, to draw water from the well. And as they stooped to dip their vessels,

Prince Fire Fade leaned and watched them from the branches of the cassia tree. And the glory of his august countenance made a brightness upon the waters of the well. So all the maidens looked up and beheld his comeliness, and were amazed. But he spoke them fairly, and desired of them a little water from their vessels. So the maidens drew him water in a jewelled cup (howbeit the jewels were clouded, because of the coldness of the well water), and they presented it to him with all reverence. Then, not drinking the water, Prince Fire Fade took the royal jewel from his neck, and holding it between his two lips he dropped it into the cup, and the cup he gave again to the maidens.

Now they saw the great jewel shining in the cup, but they could not move it, for it clung fast to the gold. So the maidens departed, skimming the water like the white birds of the offing. And they came to the Sea King's daughter, bearing the cup and the jewel in it.

And the Princess, looking at the jewel, asked them, "Is there, perchance, a stranger at the gate?"

And one of the maidens answered, "There is some one sitting in the branches of the cassia tree which is by our well."

And another said, "It is a very beautiful young man."

And another said, "He is even more glorious than our king. And he asked water of us, so we respectfully gave him water in this cup. And he drank none of it, but dropped a jewel into it from his lips. So we have brought them unto Thine Augustness, both the cup and the jewel."

Then the Princess herself took a vessel and went to draw water at the well. And her long sleeves, and certain of the folds of her august garments, floated behind her, and her head was bound with a garland of sea flowers. And coming to the well she looked up through the branches of the cassia tree. And her eyes met the eyes of Prince Fire Fade.

And presently she fetched her father, the Sea King, saying, "Father, there is a beautiful person at our gate." So the Sea King came out and welcomed Prince Fire Fade, and said, "This is the August Child of the Heaven's Sun Height." And leading him into his palace he caused the floor to be spread with eight layers of rugs of asses' skins, and eight layers of rugs of silk, and set the Prince upon them.

And that night he made a great banquet, and celebrated the betrothal of Prince Fire Fade to his daughter, the fair Jewel Princess.

And for very many days there was held high revel and rejoicing in the Sea King's palace.

But one night, as they took their ease upon the silken floor, and all the fishes of the sea brought rich dishes, and sweetmeats in vessels of gold and coral and jade to set before them, the fair Jewel Princess herself sat at Prince Fire Fade's right hand to pour the wine into his cup. And the silver scales upon the palace walls glittered in the moonlight. But Prince Fire Fade looked out across the Sea Path and thought of what had gone before, and so heaved a deep sigh.

Then the Sea King was troubled, and asked him, saying, "Wherefore dost thou sigh?" But Prince Fire Fade answered nothing.

And the fair Jewel Princess, his betrothed wife, came closer, and touched him on the breast, and said softly, "Oh, Thine Augustness, my sweet spouse, art thou not happy in our water palace, where the shadows fall green, that thou lookest so longingly across the Sea Path? Or do our maidens not please thee, who move silently, like the birds of the offing? Oh, my lord, despise me not, but tell me what is in thine heart."

Then Prince Fire Fade answered, "My lovely lady, Thine Augustness, let nothing be hidden from thee, because of our love." And he told them all the story of the fish- hook, and of his elder brother's wrath.

"And now," he said, "will the Jewel Princess give me counsel?"

Then the Jewel Princess smiled, and rose up lightly, and her hair was so long that it hung to the edge and hem of her silken red robe. And she passed to where the palace steps led down into the water. And standing upon the last step she called to the fishes of the sea, and summoned them, great and small, from far and near. So the fishes of the sea, both great and small, swam about her feet, and the water was silver with their scales. And the King's daughter cried, "O fishes of the sea, find and bring me the august fish- hook of Prince Fire Flash."

And the fishes answered, "Lady, the *Tai* is in misery, for something sticks in his throat so that he cannot eat. Perchance this may be the august fish- hook of his Augustness, Prince Fire Flash."

Then the Princess stooped down and lifted the *Tai* from the water, and with her white hand she took the lost fish- hook from his throat. And after she had washed and dabbled it for a little, she took it in to Prince Fire Fade. And he rejoiced and said, "This is indeed my brother's fish- hook. I go to restore it instantly, and we shall be reconciled." For he loved his brother.

But the fair Jewel Princess stood silent and sorrowing, for she thought, "Now will he depart and leave me lonely."

And Prince Fire Fade hastened to the water's edge, and there bestrode a valiant crocodile, who should bring him to his journey's end. And ere he went, the Sea King spoke: "Fair youth, now listen to my counsel. If thy brother sow rice upon the uplands, do thou sow thy rice low, in the water meads. But if thy brother sow his rice in the water meads, then do thou, Thine Augustness, sow thy rice upon the uplands. And I who rule the rains and the floods will continually prosper the labours of Thine Augustness. Moreover, here are two magic jewels. If thy brother should be moved by envy to attack thee, then put forth the Tide Flowing Jewel and the waters shall arise to drown him. But if thou shouldst have compassion upon him, then put forth the Tide Ebbing Jewel, and all the waters shall subside, and his life be spared."

And his Augustness Prince Fire Fade gave thanks with obeisance. And he hid the fish-hook in his long sleeve, and hung the two great jewels about his neck. Then the fair Jewel Princess came near and bade him farewell, with many tears. And the Sea King charged the crocodile, saying, "While crossing the middle of the sea, do not alarm him."

So Prince Fire Fade sat upon the crocodile's head; and in one day he came to his own place and sprang lightly to shore. And unsheathing his dagger, he hung it upon the crocodile's neck for a token.

Hereupon, Prince Fire Fade found his brother, and gave him back his own fish-hook that had been lost. Nevertheless, because of the two great jewels, which he wore in the folds of his raiment, he had everlasting dominion over his brother, and flourished in all his doings.

And, after some time, there came to Prince Fire Fade the daughter of the Sea King, the fair Jewel Princess. And she came across the Sea Path bearing in her arms a young child. And she, weeping, laid down the child at the feet of His Augustness and said, "My lord, I have brought thy son."

But Prince Fire Fade raised her up and made her welcome, and built for her a palace on the seashore, at the limit of the waves. And the palace was thatched with cormorant's feathers. So they dwelt there with the August Child.

And the fair Jewel Princess besought her lord, saying, "Sweet husband, look not on me in the dark night, for then I must take my native shape; with those of my land it is ever so. Howbeit, look not on me, lest I should be ashamed and misfortune should follow." So Prince Fire Fade promised her, and spoke many fair words of assurance.

Nevertheless, there came a night when Prince Fire Fade lay awake, and could get no rest. And, at length, when it was very dark, before the dawn, he arose and struck a light to look upon his bride as she slept. And he beheld a great scalèd dragon, with translucent eyes, which was coiled up at the couch's foot. And Prince Fire Fade cried out aloud for terror, and dropped the light. Then morning broke very grey upon the sea. And at the same instant the great dragon stirred, and from its coils the Jewel Princess lifted up her lovely head. And the green scales fell away from her like a garment. So she stood, in a white robe, with her child upon her breast. And she hung her head and wept, saying, "O Thine Augustness, my sweet spouse, I had thought to have made the Sea Path a highway between thy land and mine, that we might go and come at pleasure. But now, though I warned thee, thou hast looked upon me in the night.

Therefore, my lord, between me and thee it is farewell. I go across the Sea Path, and of this going there is no return. Take thou the August Child."

She spoke, and departed immediately upon the Sea Path, weeping and covering her face with her hair and looking back to the shore. And she was never more seen upon the Central Land of Reed Plains. Moreover, she shut the gates of the sea and closed the way to her father's palace. But the young maid, her sister, she sent to be a nurse to her babe, and because, for all that had been, she could not restrain her loving heart, she made a little song, and sent it to her lord by the maid, her sister. And the song said:

"Oh, fair are the red jewels, And fair is the string on which they are strung... Even so, fair is my babe. But brighter far, and more renowned are the white jewels, The jewels that are like my lord."

Then the husband answered, in a song which said:

"As for thee, my lady, whom I took to be my bride, To the island where lights the wild duck- the bird of the offing, I shall not forget thee till the end of my life."

The Good Thunder

Folks say that Rai- den, the Thunder, is an unloving spirit, fearful and revengeful, cruel to man. These are folks who are mortally afraid of the storm, and who hate lightning and tempest; they speak all the evil they can of Rai- den and of Rai- Taro, his son. But they are wrong.

Rai- den Sama lived in a Castle of Cloud set high in the blue heaven. He was a great and mighty god, a Lord of the Elements. Rai- Taro was his one and only son, a brave boy, and his father loved him.

In the cool of the evening Rai- den and Rai- Taro walked upon the ramparts of the Castle of Cloud, and from the ramparts they viewed the doings of men upon the Land of Reed Plains. North and South and East and West they looked. Often they laughed- oh, very often; sometimes they sighed. Sometimes Rai- Taro leaned far over the castle walls to see the children that went to and fro upon earth.

One night Rai- den Sama said to Rai- Taro, "Child, look well this night upon the doings of men!"

Rai- Taro answered, "Father, I will look well."

From the northern rampart they looked, and saw great lords and men- at- arms going forth to battle. From the southern rampart they looked, and saw priests and acolytes serving in a holy temple where the air was dim with incense, and images of gold and bronze gleamed in the twilight. From the eastern rampart they looked, and saw a lady's bower, where was a fair princess, and a troop of maidens, clad in rose colour, that made music for her. There were children there, too, playing with a little cart of flowers.

"Ah, the pretty children!" said Rai- Taro.

From the western rampart they looked, and saw a peasant toiling in a rice- field. He was weary enough and his back ached. His wife toiled with him by his side. If he was weary, it is easy to believe that she was more weary still. They were very poor and their garments were ragged.

"Have they no children?" said Rai- Taro. Rai- den shook his head.

Presently, "Have you looked well, Rai- Taro?" he said. "Have you looked well this night upon the doings of men?"

"Father," said Rai- Taro, "indeed, I have looked well."

"Then choose, my son, choose, for I send you to take up your habitation upon the earth."

"Must I go among men?" said Rai-Taro.

"My child, you must."

"I will not go with the men-at-arms," said Rai-Taro; "fighting likes me very ill."

"Oho, say you so, my son? Will you go, then, to the fair lady's bower?"

"No," said Rai-Taro, "I am a man. Neither will I have my head shaved to go and live with priests."

"What, then, do you choose the poor peasant? You will have a hard life and scanty fare, Rai-Taro."

Rai-Taro said, "They have no children. Perhaps they will love me."

"Go, go in peace," said Rai-den Sama; "for you have chosen wisely."

"How shall I go, my father?" said Rai-Taro.

"Honourably," said his father, "as it befits a Prince of High Heaven."

Now the poor peasant man toiled in his rice-field, which was at the foot of the mountain Hakusan, in the province of Ichizen. Day after day and week after week the bright sun shone. The rice-field was dry, and young rice was burnt up.

"Alack and alas!" cried the poor peasant man, "and what shall I do if my rice- crop fails? May the dear gods have mercy on all poor people!"

With that he sat himself down on a stone at the rice- field's edge and fell asleep for very weariness and sorrow.

When he woke the sky was black with clouds. It was but noonday, but it grew as dark as night. The leaves of the trees shuddered together and the birds ceased their singing.

"A storm, a storm!" cried the peasant. "Rai- den Sama goes abroad upon his black horse, beating the great drum of the Thunder. We shall have rain in plenty, thanks be."

Rain in plenty he had, sure enough, for it fell in torrents, with blinding lightning and roaring thunder.

"Oh, Rai- den Sama," said the peasant, "saving your greatness, this is even more than sufficient."

At this the bright lightning flashed anew and fell to the earth in a ball of living fire, and the heavens cracked with a mighty peal of thunder.

"Ai! Ai!" cried the poor peasant man. "Kwannon have mercy on a sinful soul, for now the Thunder Dragon has me indeed." And he lay on the ground and hid his face.

Howbeit the Thunder Dragon spared him. And soon he sat up and rubbed his eyes. The ball of fire was gone, but a babe lay upon the wet earth; a fine fresh boy with the rain upon his cheeks and his hair.

"Oh, Lady, Lady Kwannon," said the poor peasant man, "this is thy sweet mercy." And he took the boy in his arms and carried him to his own home.

As he went the rain still fell, but the sun came out in the blue sky, and every flower in the cooler air shone and lifted up its grateful head.

The peasant came to his cottage door.

"Wife, wife," he called, "I have brought you something home."

"What may it be?" said his wife.

The man answered, "Rai- Taro, the little eldest son of the Thunder."

Rai- Taro grew up straight and strong, the tallest, gayest boy of all that country- side. He was the delight of his foster- parents, and all the neighbours loved him. When he was ten years old he worked in the rice- fields like a man. He was the wonderful weather prophet.

"My father," he said, "let us do this and that, for we shall have fair weather"; or he said, "My father, let us the rather do this or that, for to- night there will be a storm," and whatever he had said, so, sure enough, it came to pass. And he brought great good fortune to the poor peasant man, and all his works prospered.

When Rai- Taro was eighteen years old all the neighbours were bidden to his birthday feast. There was plenty of good *saké*, and the good folk were merry enough; only Rai- Taro was silent and sad and sorry.

"What ails you, Rai- Taro?" said his foster-mother. "You who are wont to be the gayest of the gay, why are you silent, sad and sorry?"

"It is because I must leave you," Rai- Taro said.

"Nay," said his foster- mother, "never leave us, Rai- Taro, my son. Why would you leave us?"

"Mother, because I must," said Rai- Taro in tears.

"You have been our great good fortune; you have given us all things. What have I given you? What have I given you, Rai- Taro, my son?"

Rai- Taro answered, "Three things have you taught me- to labour, to suffer, and to love. I am more learned than the Immortals."

Then he went from them. And in the likeness of a white cloud he scaled heaven's blue height till he gained his father's castle. And Rai- den received him. The two of them stood upon the western rampart of the Castle of Cloud and looked down to earth.

The foster- mother stood weeping bitterly, but her husband took her hand.

"My dear," he said, "it will not be for long. We grow old apace."

The Black Bowl

Long ago, in a part of the country not very remote from Kioto, the great gay city, there dwelt an honest couple. In a lonely place was their cottage, upon the outskirts of a deep wood of pine trees. Folks had it that the wood was haunted. They said it was full of deceiving foxes; they said that beneath the mossy ground the elves built their kitchens; they said that long- nosed *Tengu* had tea- parties in the forest thrice a month, and that the fairies' children played at hide- and- seek there every morning before seven. Over and above all this they didn't mind saying that the honest couple were queer in their ways, that the woman was a wise woman, and that the man was a warlock- which was as may be. But sure it was that they did no harm to living soul, that they lived as poor as poor, and that they had one fair daughter. She was as neat and pretty as a princess, and her manners were very fine; but for all that she worked as hard as a boy in the rice- fields, and within doors she was the housewife indeed, for she washed and cooked and drew water. She went barefoot in a grey homespun gown, and tied her back hair with a tough wistaria tendril. Brown she was and thin, but the sweetest beggar- maid that ever made shift with a bed of dry moss and no supper.

By- and- by the good man her father dies, and the wise woman her mother sickens within the year, and soon she lies in a corner of the cottage waiting for her end, with the maid near her crying bitter tears.

"Child," says the mother, "do you know you are as pretty as a princess?"

"Am I that?" says the maid, and goes on with her crying.

"Do you know that your manners are fine?" says the mother.

"Are they, then?" says the maid, and goes on with her crying.

"My own baby," says the mother, "could you stop your crying a minute and listen to me?"

So the maid stopped crying and put her head close by her mother's on the poor pillow.

"Now listen," says the mother, "and afterwards remember. It is a bad thing for a poor girl to be pretty. If she is pretty and lonely and innocent, none but the gods will help her. They will help you, my poor child, and I have thought of a way besides. Fetch me the great black rice- bowl from the shelf."

The girl fetched it.

"See, now, I put it on your head and all your beauty is hidden away."

"Alack, mother," said the poor child, "it is heavy."

"It will save you from what is heavier to bear," said the mother. "If you love me, promise me that you will not move it till the time comes."

"I promise! I promise! But how shall I know when the time comes?"

"That you shall know.... And now help me outside, for the sweet morning dawns and I've a fancy to see the fairies' children once again, as they run in the forest."

So the child, having the black bowl upon her head, held her mother in her arms in a grassy place near the great trees, and presently they saw the fairies' children threading their way between the dark trunks as they played at hide- and- seek. Their bright garments fluttered, and they laughed lightly as they went. The mother smiled to see them; before seven she died very sweetly as she smiled.

When her little store of rice was done, the maid with the wooden bowl knew well enough that she must starve or go and find more. So first she tended her father's and mother's graves and poured water for the dead, as is meet, and recited many a holy text.

Then she bound on her sandals, kilted her grey skirts to show her scarlet petticoat, tied her household gods in a blue printed handkerchief, and set out all alone to seek her fortunes, the brave girl!

For all her slenderness and pretty feet she was a rarely odd sight, and soon she was to know it. The great black bowl covered her head and shadowed her face. As she went through a village two women looked up from washing in the stream, stared and laughed.

"It's a boggart come alive," says one.

"Out upon her," cries the other, "for a shameless wench! Out upon her false modesty to roam the country thus with her head in a black bowl, as who should cry aloud to every passing man, 'Come and see what is hidden!' It is enough to make a wholesome body sick."

On went the poor maid, and sometimes the children pelted her with mud and pebbles for sport. Sometimes she was handled roughly by village louts, who scoffed and caught at her dress as she went; they even laid hands upon the bowl itself and sought to drag it from her head by force. But they only played at that game once, for the bowl stung them as fiercely as if it had been a nettle, and the bullies ran away howling.

The beggar- maiden might seek her fortune, but it was very hard to find. She might ask for work; but see, would she get it? None were wishful to employ a girl with a black bowl on her head.

At last, on a fine day when she was tired out, she sat her upon a stone and began to cry as if her heart would break. Down rolled her tears from under the black bowl. They rolled down her cheeks and reached her white chin.

A wandering ballad- singer passed that way, with his *biwa* slung across his back. He had a sharp eye and marked the tears upon the maid's white chin. It was all he could see of her face, and, "Oh, girl with the black bowl on your head," quoth he, "why do you sit weeping by the roadside?"

"I weep," she answered, "because the world is hard. I am hungry and tired.... No one will give me work or pay me money."

"Now that's unfortunate," said the ballad- singer, for he had a kind heart; "but I haven't a *rin* of my own, or it would be yours. Indeed I am sorry for you. In the circumstances the best I can do for you is to make you a little song." With that he whips his *biwa* round, thrums on it with his fingers and starts as easy as you please. "To the tears on your white chin," he says, and sings:

"*The white cherry blooms by the roadside, How black is the canopy of cloud! The wild cherry droops by the roadside, Beware of the black canopy of cloud. Hark, hear the rain, hear the rainfall From the black canopy of cloud. Alas, the wild cherry, its sweet flowers are marred,Marred are the sweet flowers, forlorn on the spray!*"

"Sir, I do not understand your song," said the girl with the bowl on her head.

"Yet it is plain enough," said the ballad-singer, and went his way. He came to the house of a passing rich farmer. In he went, and they asked him to sing before the master of the house.

"With all the will in the world," says the ballad- singer. "I will sing him a new song that I have just made." So he sang of the wild cherry and the great black cloud.

When he had made an end, "Tell us the interpretation of your song," says the master of the house.

"With all the will in the world," quoth the ballad- singer. "The wild cherry is the face of a maiden whom I saw sitting by the wayside. She wore a great black wooden bowl upon her head, which is the great black cloud in my song, and from under it her tears flowed like rain, for I saw the drops upon her white chin. And she said that she wept for hunger, and

74

because no one would give her work nor pay her money."

"Now I would I might help the poor girl with the bowl on her head," said the master of the house.

"That you may if you wish," quoth the ballad- singer. "She sits but a stone's throw from your gate."

The long and short of it was that the maid was put to labour in the rich farmer's harvest-fields. All the day long she worked in the waving rice, with her grey skirts kilted and her sleeves bound back with cords. All day long she plied the sickle, and the sun shone down upon the black bowl; but she had food to eat and good rest at night, and was well content.

She found favour in her master's eyes, and he kept her in the fields till all the harvest was gathered in. Then he took her into his house, where there was plenty for her to do, for his wife was but sickly. Now the maiden lived well and happily as a bird, and went singing about her labours. And every night she thanked the august gods for her good fortune. Still she wore the black bowl upon her head.

At the New Year time, "Bustle, bustle," says the farmer's wife; "scrub and cook and sew; put your best foot foremost, my dear, for we must have the house look at its very neatest."

"To be sure, and with all my heart," says the girl, and she put her back into the work; "but, mistress," she says, "if I may be so bold as to ask, are we having a party, or what?"

"Indeed we are, and many of them," says the farmer's wife. "My son that is in Kioto, the great and gay, is coming home for a visit."

Presently home he comes, the handsome young man. Then the neighbours were called in, and great was the merry- making. They feasted and they danced, they jested and they sang, many a bowl of good red rice they ate, and many a cup of good *saké* they drank. All this time the girl, with bowl on her head, plied her work modestly in the kitchen, and well out of the way she was- the farmer's wife saw to that, good soul! All the same, one fine day the company called for more wine, and the wine was done, so the son of the house takes up the *saké* bottle and goes with it himself to the kitchen. What should he see there but the maiden sitting upon a pile of faggots, and fanning the kitchen fire with a split bamboo fan!

"My life, but I must see what is under that black bowl," says the handsome young man to himself. And sure enough he made it his daily care, and peeped as much as he could, which was not very much; but seemingly it was enough for him, for he thought no more of Kioto, the great and gay, but stayed at home to do his courting.

His father laughed and his mother fretted, the neighbours held up their hands, all to no purpose.

"Oh, dear, dear maiden with the wooden bowl, she shall be my bride and no other. I must and will have her," cried the impetuous young man, and very soon he fixed the wedding- day himself.

When the time came, the young maidens of the village went to array the bride. They dressed her in a fair and costly robe of white brocade, and in trailing *hakama* of scarlet silk, and on her shoulders they hung a cloak of blue and purple and gold. They chattered, but as for the bride she said never a word. She was sad because she brought her bridegroom nothing, and because his parents were sore at his choice of a beggar- maid. She said nothing, but the tears glistened on her white chin.

"Now off with the ugly old bowl," cried the maidens; "it is time to dress the bride's hair and to do it with golden combs." So they laid hands to the bowl and would have lifted it away, but they could not move it.

"Try again," they said, and tugged at it with all their might. But it would not stir.

"There's witchcraft in it," they said; "try a third time." They tried a third time, and still the bowl stuck fast, but it gave out fearsome moans and cries.

"Ah! Let be, let be for pity's sake," said the poor bride, "for you make my head ache."

They were forced to lead her as she was to the bridegroom's presence.

"My dear, I am not afraid of the wooden bowl," said the young man.

So they poured the *sake* from the silver flagon, and from the silver cup the two of them drank the mystic "Three Times Three" that made them man and wife.

Then the black bowl burst asunder with a loud noise, and fell to the ground in a thousand pieces. With it fell a shower of silver and gold, and pearls and rubies and emeralds, and every jewel of price. Great was the astonishment of the company as they gazed upon a dowry that for a princess would have been rich and rare.

But the bridegroom looked into the bride's face. "My dear," he said, "there are no jewels that shine like your eyes."

The Star Lovers

All you that are true lovers, I beseech you pray the gods for fair weather upon the seventh night of the seventh moon.

For patience' sake and for dear love's sake, pray, and be pitiful that upon that night there may be neither rain, nor hail, nor cloud, nor thunder, nor creeping mist.

Hear the sad tale of the Star Lovers and give them your prayers.

The Weaving Maiden was the daughter of a Deity of Light. Her dwelling was upon the shore of the Milky Way, which is the Bright River of Heaven. All the day long she sat at her loom and plied her shuttle, weaving the gay garments of the gods. Warp and woof, hour by hour the coloured web grew till it lay fold on fold piled at her feet. Still she never ceased her labour, for she was afraid. She had heard a saying:

"Sorrow, age- long sorrow, shall come upon the Weaving Maiden when she leaves her loom."

So she laboured, and the gods had garments to spare. But she herself, poor maiden, was ill-clad; she recked nothing of her attire or of the jewels that her father gave her. She went barefoot, and let her hair hang down unconfined. Ever and anon a long lock fell upon the loom, and back she flung it over her shoulder. She did not play with the children of Heaven, or take her pleasure with celestial youths and maidens. She did not love or weep. She was neither glad nor sorry. She sat weaving, weaving... and wove her being into the many- coloured web.

Now her father, the Deity of Light, grew angry. He said, "Daughter, you weave too much."

"It is my duty," she said.

"At your age to talk of duty!" said her father. "Out upon you!"

"Wherefore are you displeased with me, my father?" she said, and her fingers plied the shuttle.

"Are you a stock or a stone, or a pale flower by the wayside?"

"Nay," she said, "I am none of these."

"Then leave your loom, my child, and live; take your pleasure, be as others are."

"And wherefore should I be as others are?" she said.

"Never dare to question me. Come, will you leave your loom?"

She said, "Sorrow, age- long sorrow, shall come upon the Weaving Maiden when she leaves her loom."

"A foolish saying," cried her father, "not worthy of credence. What do we know of age-long sorrow? Are we not gods?" With that he took her shuttle from her hand gently, and covered the loom with a cloth. And he caused her to be very richly attired, and they put jewels upon her and garlanded her head with flowers of Paradise. And her father gave her for spouse the Herd Boy of Heaven, who tended his flocks upon the banks of the Bright River.

Now the Maiden was changed indeed. Her eyes were stars and her lips were ruddy. She went dancing and singing all the day. Long hours she played with the children of Heaven, and she took her pleasure with the celestial youths and maidens. Lightly she went; her feet were shod with silver. Her lover, the Herd Boy, held her by the hand. She laughed so that the very gods laughed with her, and High Heaven re- echoed with sounds of mirth. She was careless; little did she think of duty or of the garments of the gods. As for her loom, she never went near it from one moon's end to another.

"I have my life to live," she said; "I'll weave it into a web no more."

And the Herd Boy, her lover, clasped her in his arms. Her face was all tears and smiles, and she hid it on his breast. So she lived her life. But her father, the Deity of Light, was angry.

"It is too much," he said. "Is the girl mad? She will become the laughing- stock of Heaven. Besides, who is to weave the new spring garments of the gods?"

Three times he warned his daughter.

Three times she laughed softly and shook her head.

"Your hand opened the door, my father," she said, "but of a surety no hand either of god or of mortal can shut it."

He said, "You shall find it otherwise to your cost." And he banished the Herd Boy for ever and ever to the farther side of the Bright River. The magpies flew together, from far and near, and they spread their wings for a frail bridge across the river, and the Herd Boy went over by the frail bridge. And immediately the magpies flew away to the ends of the earth and the Weaving Maiden could not follow. She was the saddest thing in Heaven. Long, long she stood upon the shore, and held out her arms to the Herd Boy, who tended his oxen desolate and in tears. Long, long she lay and wept upon the sand. Long, long she brooded, looking on the ground.

She arose and went to her loom. She cast aside the cloth that covered it. She took her shuttle in her hand.

"Age- long sorrow," she said, "age- long sorrow!" Presently she dropped the shuttle. "Ah," she moaned, "the pain of it," and she leaned her head against the loom.

But in a little while she said, "Yet I would not be as once I was. I did not love or weep, I was neither glad nor sorry. Now I love and I weep- I am glad, and I am sorry."

Her tears fell like rain, but she took up the shuttle and laboured diligently, weaving the garments of the gods. Sometimes the web was grey with grief, sometimes it was rosy with dreams. The gods were fain to go strangely clad. The Maiden's father, the Deity of Light, for once was well pleased.

"That is my good, diligent child," he said. "Now you are quiet and happy."

"The quiet of dark despair," she said. "Happy! I am the saddest thing in Heaven."

"I am sorry," said the Deity of Light; "what shall I do?"

"Give me back my lover."

"Nay, child, that I cannot do. He is banished for ever and ever by the decree of a Deity, that cannot be broken."

"I knew it," she said.

"Yet something I can do. Listen. On the seventh day of the seventh moon, I will summon the magpies together from the ends of the earth, and they shall be a bridge over the Bright River of Heaven, so that the Weaving Maiden shall lightly cross to the waiting Herd Boy on the farther shore."

So it was. On the seventh day of the seventh moon came the magpies from far and near. And they spread their wings for a frail bridge. And the Weaving Maiden went over by the frail bridge. Her eyes were like stars, and her heart like a bird in her bosom. And the Herd Boy was there to meet her upon the farther shore.

And so it is still, oh, true lovers- upon the seventh day of the seventh moon these two keep their tryst. Only if the rain falls with thunder and cloud and hail, and the Bright River of Heaven is swollen and swift, the magpies cannot make a bridge for the Weaving Maiden. Alack, the dreary time!

Therefore, true lovers, pray the gods for fair weather.

Horaizan

Jofuku was the Wise Man of China. Many books he read, and he never forgot what was in them. All the characters he knew as he knew the lines in the palm of his hand. He learned secrets from birds and beasts, and herbs and flowers and trees, and rocks and metals. He knew magic and poetry and philosophy. He grew full of years and wisdom. All the people honoured him; but he was not happy, for he had a word written upon his heart.

The word was *Mutability*. It was with him day and night, and sorely it troubled him. Moreover, in the days of Jofuku a tyrant ruled over China, and he made the Wise Man's life a burden.

"Jofuku," he said, "teach the nightingales of my wood to sing me the songs of the Chinese poets."

Jofuku could not do it for all his wisdom.

"Alas, liege," he said, "ask me another thing and I will give it you, though it cost me the blood of my heart."

"Have a care," said the Emperor, "look to your ways. Wise men are cheap in China; am I one to be dishonoured?"

"Ask me another thing," said the Wise Man.

"Well, then, scent me the peony with the scent of the jessamine. The peony is brilliant, imperial; the jessamine is small, pale, foolish. Nevertheless, its perfume is sweet. Scent me the peony with the scent of the jessamine."

But Jofuku stood silent and downcast.

"By the gods," cried the Emperor, "this wise man is a fool! Here, some of you, off with his head."

"Liege," said the Wise Man, "spare me my life and I will set sail for Horaizan where grows the herb Immortality. I will pluck this herb and bring it back to you again, that you may live and reign for ever."

The Emperor considered.

"Well, go," he said, "and linger not, or it will be the worse for you."

Jofuku went and found brave companions to go with him on the great adventure, and he manned a junk with the most famous mariners of China, and he took stores on board, and gold; and when he had made all things ready he set sail in the seventh month, about the time of the full moon.

The Emperor himself came down to the seashore.

"Speed, speed, Wise Man," he said; "fetch me the herb Immortality, and see that you do it presently. If you return without it, you and your companions shall die the death."

"Farewell, liege," called Jofuku from the junk. So they went with a fair wind for their white sails. The boards creaked, the ropes quivered, the water splashed against the junk's side, the sailors sang as they steered a course eastward, the brave companions were merry. But the Wise Man of China looked forward and looked back, and was sad because of the word written upon his heart- *Mutability*.

The junk of Jofuku was for many days upon the wild sea, steering a course eastwards. He and the sailors and the brave companions suffered many things. The great heat burnt them, and the great cold froze them. Hungry and thirsty they were, and some of them fell sick and died. More were slain in a fight with pirates. Then came the dread typhoon, and mountain waves that swept the junk. The masts and the sails were washed away with the rich stores, and the gold was lost for ever. Drowned were the famous mariners, and the brave companions every one. Jofuku was left alone.

In the grey dawn he looked up. Far to the east he saw a mountain, very faint, the colour of pearl, and on the mountain top there grew a tree, tall, with spreading branches. The Wise Man murmured:

"The Island of Horaizan is east of the east, and there is Fusan, the Wonder Mountain. On the heights of Fusan there grows a tree whose branches hide the Mysteries of Life."

Jofuku lay weak and weary and could not lift a finger. Nevertheless, the junk glided nearer and nearer to the shore. Still and blue grew the waters of the sea, and Jofuku saw the bright green grass and the many- coloured flowers of the island. Soon there came troops of young men and maidens bearing garlands and singing songs of welcome; and they waded out into the water and drew the junk to land. Jofuku was aware of the sweet and spicy odours that clung to their garments and their hair. At their invitation he left the junk, which drifted away and was no more seen.

He said, "I have come to Horaizan the Blest." Looking up he saw that the trees were full of birds with blue and golden feathers. The birds filled the air with delightful melody. On all sides there hung the orange and the citron, the persimmon and the pomegranate, the peach and the plum and the loquat. The ground at his feet was as a rich brocade, embroidered with every flower that is. The happy dwellers in Horaizan took him by the hands and spoke lovingly to him.

"How strange it is," said Jofuku, "I do not feel my old age any more."

"What is old age?" they said.

"Neither do I feel any pain."

"Now what is pain?" they said.

"The word is no longer written on my heart."

"What word do you speak of, beloved?"

"*Mutability* is the word."

"And what may be its interpretation?"

"Tell me," said the Wise Man, "is this death?"

"We have never heard of death," said the inhabitants of Horaizan.

The Wise Man of Japan was Wasobiobe. He was full as wise as the Wise Man of China. He was not old but young. The people honoured him and loved him. Often he was happy enough.

It was his pleasure to venture alone in a frail boat out to sea, there to meditate in the wild and watery waste. Once as he did this it chanced that he fell asleep in his boat, and he slept all night long, while his boat drifted out to the eastward. So, when he awoke in the bright light of morning, he found himself beneath the shadow of Fusan, the Wonder Mountain. His boat lay in the waters of a river of Horaizan, and he steered her amongst the flowering iris and the lotus, and sprang on shore.

"The sweetest spot in the world!" he said. "I think I have come to Horaizan the Blest."

Soon came the youths and maidens of the island, and with them the Wise Man of China, as young and as happy as they.

"Welcome, welcome, dear brother," they cried, "welcome to the Island of Eternal Youth."

When they had given him to eat of the delicious fruit of the island, they laid them down upon a bank of flowers to hear sweet music. Afterwards they wandered in the woods and groves. They rode and hunted, or bathed in the warm sea- water. They feasted and enjoyed every delightful pleasure. So the long day lingered, and there was no night, for there was no need of sleep, there was no weariness and no pain.

The Wise Man of Japan came to the Wise Man of China. He said:

"I cannot find my boat."

"What matter, brother?" said Jofuku. "You want no boat here."

"Indeed, my brother, I do. I want my boat to take me home. I am sick for home. There's the truth."

"Are you not happy in Horaizan?"

"No, for I have a word written upon my heart. The word is *Humanity*. Because of it I am troubled and have no peace."

"Strange," said the Wise Man of China. "Once I too had a word written on my heart. The word was *Mutability*, but I have forgotten what it means. Do you too forget."

"Nay, I can never forget," said the Wise Man of Japan.

He sought out the Crane, who is a great traveller, and besought her, "Take me home to my own land."

"Alas," the Crane said, "if I did so you would die. This is the Island of Eternal Youth; do you know you have been here for a hundred years? If you go away you will feel old age and weariness and pain, then you will die."

"No matter," said Wasobiobe, "take me home."

Then the Crane took him on her strong back and flew with him. Day and night she flew and never tarried and never tired. At last she said, "Do you see the shore?"

And he said, "I see it. Praise be to the gods."

She said, "Where shall I carry you?... You have but a little time to live."

"Good Crane, upon the dear sand of my country, under the spreading pine, there sits a poor fisherman mending his net. Take me to him that I may die in his arms."

So the Crane laid Wasobiobe at the poor fisherman's feet. And the fisherman raised him in his arms. And Wasobiobe laid his head against the fisherman's humble breast.

"I might have lived for ever," he said, "but for the word that is written on my heart."

"What word?" said the fisherman.

"*Humanity* is the word," the Wise Man murmured. "I am grown old- hold me closer. Ah, the pain...." He gave a great cry.

Afterwards he smiled. Then his breath left him with a sigh, and he was dead.

"It is the way of all flesh," said the fisherman.

Reflections

Long enough ago there dwelt within a day's journey of the city of Kioto a gentleman of simple mind and manners, but good estate. His wife, rest her soul, had been dead these many years, and the good man lived in great peace and quiet with his only son. They kept clear of women- kind, and knew nothing at all either of their winning or their bothering ways. They had good steady men- servants in their house, and never set eyes on a pair of long sleeves or a scarlet *obi* from morning till night.

The truth is that they were as happy as the day is long. Sometimes they laboured in the rice- fields. Other days they went a- fishing. In the spring, forth they went to admire the cherry flower or the plum, and later they set out to view the iris or the peony or the lotus, as the case might be. At these times they would drink a little *saké*, and twist their blue and white *tenegui* about their heads and be as jolly as you please, for there was no one to say them nay. Often enough they came home by lantern light. They wore their oldest clothes, and were mighty irregular at their meals.

But the pleasures of life are fleeting- more's the pity!- and presently the father felt old age creeping upon him.

One night, as he sat smoking and warming his hands over the charcoal, "Boy," says he, "it's high time you got married."

"Now the gods forbid!" cries the young man. "Father, what makes you say such terrible things? Or are you joking? You must be joking," he says.

"I'm not joking at all," says the father; "I never spoke a truer word, and that you'll know soon enough."

"But, father, I am mortally afraid of women."

"And am I not the same?" says the father. "I'm sorry for you, my boy."

"Then what for must I marry?" says the son.

"In the way of nature I shall die before long, and you'll need a wife to take care of you."

Now the tears stood in the young man's eyes when he heard this, for he was tender-hearted; but all he said was, "I can take care of myself very well."

"That's the very thing you cannot," says his father.

The long and short of it was that they found the young man a wife. She was young, and as pretty as a picture. Her name was Tassel, just that, or Fusa, as they say in her language.

After they had drunk down the "Three Times Three" together and so became man and wife, they stood alone, the young man looking hard at the girl. For the life of him he did not know what to say to her. He took a bit of her sleeve and stroked it with his hand. Still he said nothing and looked mighty foolish. The girl turned red, turned pale, turned red again, and burst into tears.

"Honourable Tassel, don't do that, for the dear gods' sake," says the young man.

"I suppose you don't like me," sobs the girl. "I suppose you don't think I'm pretty."

"My dear," he says, "you're prettier than the bean- flower in the field; you're prettier than the little bantam hen in the farm- yard; you're prettier than the rose carp in the pond. I hope you'll be happy with my father and me."

At this she laughed a little and dried her eyes. "Get on another pair of *hakama*," she says, "and give me those you've got on you; there's a great hole in them- I was noticing it all the time of the wedding!"

Well, this was not a bad beginning, and taking one thing with another they got on pretty well, though of course things were not as they had been in that blessed time when the young man and his father did not set eyes upon a pair of long sleeves or an *obi* from morning till night.

By and by, in the way of nature, the old man died. It is said he made a very good end, and left that in his strong- box which made his son the richest man in the country- side. But this was no comfort at all to the poor young man, who mourned his father with all his heart. Day and night he paid reverence to the tomb. Little sleep or rest he got, and little heed he gave to his wife, Mistress Tassel, and her whimsies, or even to the delicate dishes she set before him. He grew thin and pale, and she, poor maid, was at her wits' end to know what to do with him. At last she said, "My dear, and how would it be if you were to go to Kioto for a little?"

"And what for should I do that?" he says.

It was on the tip of her tongue to answer, "To enjoy yourself," but she saw it would never do to say that.

"Oh," she says, "as a kind of a duty. They say every man that loves his country should see Kioto; and besides, you might give an eye to the fashions, so as to tell me what like they are when you get home. My things," she says, "are sadly behind the times! I'd like well enough to know what people are wearing!"

"I've no heart to go to Kioto," says the young man, "and if I had, it's the planting- out time of the rice, and the thing's not to be done, so there's an end of it."

All the same, after two days he bids his wife get out his best *hakama* and *haouri*, and to make up his *bento* for a journey. "I'm thinking of going to Kioto," he tells her.

"Well, I am surprised," says Mistress Tassel. "And what put such an idea into your head, if I may ask?"

"I've been thinking it's a kind of duty," says the young man.

"Oh, indeed," says Mistress Tassel to this, and nothing more, for she had some grains of sense. And the next morning as ever was she packs her husband off bright and early for Kioto, and betakes herself to some little matter of house cleaning she has on hand.

The young man stepped out along the road, feeling a little better in his spirits, and before long he reached Kioto. It is likely he saw many things to wonder at. Amongst temples and palaces he went. He saw castles and gardens, and marched up and down fine streets of shops, gazing about him with his eyes wide open, and his mouth too, very like, for he was a simple soul.

At length, one fine day he came upon a shop full of metal mirrors that glittered in the sunshine.

"Oh, the pretty silver moons!" says the simple soul to himself. And he dared to come near and take up a mirror in his hand.

The next minute he turned as white as rice and sat him down on the seat in the shop door, still holding the mirror in his hand and looking into it.

"Why, father," he said, "how did you come here? You are not dead, then? Now the dear gods be praised for that! Yet I could have sworn- But no matter, since you are here alive and well. You are something pale still, but how young you look. You move your lips, father, and seem to speak, but I do not hear you. You'll come home with me, dear, and live with us just as you used to do? You smile, you smile, that is well."

"Fine mirrors, my young gentleman," said the shopman, "the best that can be made, and that's one of the best of the lot you have there. I see you are a judge."

The young man clutched his mirror tight and sat staring stupidly enough no doubt. He trembled. "How much?" he whispered. "Is it for sale?" He was in a taking lest his father should be snatched from him.

"For sale it is, indeed, most noble sir," said the shopman, "and the price is a trifle, only two *bu*. It's almost giving it away I am, as you'll understand."

"Two *bu*- only two *bu*! Now the gods be praised for this their mercy!" cried the happy young man. He smiled from ear to ear, and he had the purse out of his girdle, and the money out of his purse, in a twinkling.

Now it was the shopman who wished he had asked three *bu* or even five. All the same he put a good face upon it, and packed the mirror in a fine white box and tied it up with green cords.

"Father," said the young man, when he had got away with it, "before we set out for home we must buy some gauds for the young woman there, my wife, you know."

Now, for the life of him, he could not have told why, but when he came to his home the young man never said a word to Mistress Tassel about buying his old father for two *bu* in the Kioto shop. That was where he made his mistake, as things turned out.

She was as pleased as you like with her coral hair- pins, and her fine new *obi* from Kioto. "And I'm glad to see him so well and so happy," she said to herself; "but I must say he's been mighty quick to get over his sorrow after all. But men are just like children." As for her husband, unbeknown to her he took a bit of green silk from her treasure- box and spread it in the cupboard of the *toko no ma*. There he placed the mirror in its box of white wood.

Every morning early and every evening late, he went to the cupboard of the *toko no ma* and spoke with his father. Many a jolly talk they had and many a hearty laugh together, and the son was the happiest young man of all that country- side, for he was a simple soul.

But Mistress Tassel had a quick eye and a sharp ear, and it was not long before she marked her husband's new ways.

"What for does he go so often to the *toko no ma*," she asked herself, "and what has he got there? I should be glad enough to know." Not being one to suffer much in silence, she very soon asked her husband these same things.

He told her the truth, the good young man. "And now I have my dear old father home again, I'm as happy as the day is long," he says.

"H'm," she says.

"And wasn't two *bu* cheap," he says, "and wasn't it a strange thing altogether?"

"Cheap, indeed," says she, "and passing strange; and why, if I may ask," she says, "did you say nought of all this at the first?"

The young man grew red.

"Indeed, then, I cannot tell you, my dear," he says. "I'm sorry, but I don't know," and with that he went out to his work.

Up jumped Mistress Tassel the minute his back was turned, and to the *toko no ma* she flew on the wings of the wind and flung open the doors with a clang.

"My green silk for sleeve- linings!" she cried at once; "but I don't see any old father here, only a white wooden box. What can he keep in it?"

She opened the box quickly enough.

"What an odd flat shining thing!" she said, and, taking up the mirror, looked into it.

For a moment she said nothing at all, but the great tears of anger and jealousy stood in her pretty eyes, and her face flushed from forehead to chin.

"A woman!" she cried, "a woman! So that is his secret! He keeps a woman in this cupboard. A woman, very young and very pretty- no, not pretty at all, but she thinks herself so. A dancing- girl from Kioto, I'll be bound; ill- tempered too- her face is scarlet; and oh, how she frowns, nasty little spitfire.

Ah, who could have thought it of him? Ah, it's a miserable girl I am- and I've cooked his *daikon* and mended his *hakama* a hundred times. Oh! oh! oh!"

With that, she threw the mirror into its case, and slammed- to the cupboard door upon it. Herself she flung upon the mats, and cried and sobbed as if her heart would break.

In comes her husband.

"I've broken the thong of my sandal," says he, "and I've come to- - But what in the world?" and in an instant he was down on his knees beside Mistress Tassel doing what he could to comfort her, and to get her face up from the floor where she kept it.

"Why, what is it, my own darling?" says he.

"*Your* own darling!" she answers very fierce through her sobs; and "I want to go home," she cries.

"But, my sweet, you are at home, and with your own husband."

"Pretty husband!" she says, "and pretty goings- on, with a woman in the cupboard! A hateful, ugly woman that thinks herself beautiful; and she has *my* green sleeve- linings there with her to boot."

"Now, what's all this about women and sleeve- linings? Sure you wouldn't grudge poor old father that little green rag for his bed? Come, my dear, I'll buy you twenty sleeve- linings."

At that she jumped to her feet and fairly danced with rage.

"Old father! old father! old father!" she screamed; "am I a fool or a child? I saw the woman with my own eyes."

The poor young man didn't know whether he was on his head or his heels. "Is it possible that my father is gone?" he said, and he took the mirror from the *toko no ma*.

"That's well; still the same old father that I bought for two *bu*. You seem worried, father; nay, then, smile as I do. There, that's well."

Mistress Tassel came like a little fury and snatched the mirror from his hand. She gave but one look into it and hurled it to the other end of the room. It made such a clang against the woodwork, that servants and neighbours came rushing in to see what was the matter.

"It is my father," said the young man. "I bought him in Kioto for two *bu*."

"He keeps a woman in the cupboard who has stolen my green sleeve- linings," sobbed the wife.

After this there was a great to- do. Some of the neighbours took the man's part and some the woman's, with such a clatter and chatter and noise as never was; but settle the thing they could not, and none of them would look into the mirror, because they said it was bewitched.

They might have gone on the way they were till doomsday, but that one of them said, "Let us ask the Lady Abbess, for she is a wise woman." And off they all went to do what they might have done sooner.

The Lady Abbess was a pious woman, the head of a convent of holy nuns. She was the great one at prayers and meditations and at mortifyings of the flesh, and she was the clever one, none the less, at human affairs. They took her the mirror, and she held it in her hands and looked into it for a long time. At last she spoke:

"This poor woman," she said, touching the mirror, "for it's as plain as daylight that it is a woman- this poor woman was so troubled in her mind at the disturbance that she caused in a quiet house, that she has taken vows, shaved her head, and become a holy nun. Thus she is in her right place here. I will keep her, and instruct her in prayers and meditations. Go you home, my children; forgive and forget, be friends."

Then all the people said, "The Lady Abbess is the wise woman."

And she kept the mirror in her treasure.

Mistress Tassel and her husband went home hand in hand.

"So I was right, you see, after all," she said.

"Yes, yes, my dear," said the simple young man, "of course. But I was wondering how my old father would get on at the holy convent. He was never much of a one for religion."

The Story of Susa, the Impetuous

When Izanagi, the Lord who Invites, turned his back upon the unclean place, and bade farewell to Yomi, the World of the Dead, whither he had journeyed upon a quest, he beheld once more the Land of Fresh Rice Ears, and was glad. And he rested by the side of a clear river that he might perform purification.

And Izanagi- no- Mikoto bathed in the upper reach. But he said, "The water of the upper reach is too rapid." Then he bathed in the lower reach; but he said, "The water of the lower reach is too sluggish." So he went down for the third time and bathed in the middle reach of the river. And as the water dropped from his beautiful countenance there were created three sublime deities- Ama Terassu, the Glory of High Heaven; Tsuki-Yomi- no- Kami, the Moon- Night-Possessor; and Susa, the Impetuous, the Lord of the Sea.

Then Izanagi- no- Mikoto rejoiced, saying, "Behold the three august children that are mine, who shall also be illustrious for ever." And, taking the great string of jewels from his neck, he bestowed it upon Ama Terassu, the Glorious, and said to her, "Do Thine

Augustness rule the Plain of High Heaven, shining in thy beauty by day." So she took the august jewels and hid them in the storehouse of the gods.

And the Lord of Invitation commanded Tsuki- Yomi- no- Kami, saying, "Do Thine Augustness rule the Dominion of the Night." Now this was a youth of a fair and pleasant countenance.

And to the youngest of the deities, his Augustness the Lord Izanagi gave the Sea Plain.

So Ama Terassu ruled the day, and Tsuki-Yomi- no- Kami softly ruled the night. But Susa, the Impetuous, flung himself upon the ground and violently wept, for he said, "Ah, miserable, to dwell for ever upon the confines of the cold sea!" So he ceased not in his weeping, and took the moisture of the valley for his tears, so that the green places were withered and the rivers and streams were dried up. And evil deities increased and flourished, and as they swarmed upon the earth their noise was as the noise of flies in the fifth moon; and far and wide there arose portents of woe.

Then his father, the Lord of Invitation, came and stood terribly by him and said, "What is this that I do see and hear? Why dost thou not rule the dominions with which I charged thee, but lie here, like a child, with tears and wailings? Answer."

And Susa, the Impetuous, answered, "I wail because I am in misery and love not this place, but would depart to my mother who rules the Nether Distant Land, who is called the Queen of Yomi, the World of the Dead."

Then Izanagi was wroth and expelled him with a divine expulsion, and charged him that he should depart and show his face no more.

And Susa, the Impetuous, answered, "So be it. But first I will ascend to High Heaven to take leave of Her Augustness, my sister, who is the Glory of Heaven, and then I will depart."

So he went up to Heaven with a noise and a great speed, and at his going all the mountains shook and every land and country quaked. And Ama Terassu, the Light of Heaven, she also trembled at his coming, and said, "This coming of His Augustness, my brother, is of no good intent, but to lay hold of mine inheritance, and to take it by force. For this alone does he invade the fastness of High Heaven."

And forthwith she divided the hair that hung upon her shoulders and rolled it in two august bunches to the left and to the right, and adorned it with jewels. So she made her head like the head of a young warrior. And she slung upon her back a great bow and a quiver of arrows, one thousand and five hundred arrows, and she took in her hand a bamboo staff and brandished it and stamped upon the ground with her armed feet, so that the earth flew like powdered snow. So she came to the bank of the Tranquil River of Heaven and stood valiantly, like unto a mighty man, and waited.

And Susa, the Impetuous, spoke from the farther bank: "My lovely sister, Thine Augustness, why comest thou thus armed against me?"

And she answered, "Nay, but wherefore ascendest thou hither?"

And Susa replied, "There is nothing evil in my mind. Because I desired to dwell in the Land of Yomi, therefore has my father deigned to expel me with a divine expulsion, and I thought to take leave of thee, and so I have ascended hither. I have no evil intention."

And she, bending her great eyes on him, said "Swear."

And he swore, by the ten- grasp sword that was girded on him, and after that he swore by the jewels in her hair. Then she suffered him to cross over the Tranquil River of Heaven, and also to cross over the Floating Bridge. So Susa, the Impetuous, entered the dominions of his sister, the Sun Goddess.

But his wild spirit never ceased to chafe. And he pillaged the fair lands of Ama Terassu and broke down the divisions of the rice-fields which she had planted, and filled in the ditches. Still the Light of Heaven upbraided him not, but said, "His Augustness, my brother, believes that the land should not be wasted by ditches and divisions, and that rice should be sown everywhere, without distinction." But notwithstanding her soft words Susa, the Impetuous, continued in his evil ways and became more and more violent.

Now, as the great Sun Goddess sat with her maidens in the awful Weaving Hall of High Heaven, seeing to the weaving of the august garments of the gods, her brother made a mighty chasm in the roof of the Weaving Hall, and through the chasm he let down a heavenly piebald horse. And the horse fled hither and thither in terror, and wrought great havoc amongst the looms and amongst the weaving maidens. And Susa himself followed like a rushing tempest and like a storm of waters flooding the hall, and all was confusion and horror. And in the press the Sun Goddess was wounded with her golden shuttle. So with a cry she fled from High Heaven and hid herself in a cave; and she rolled a rock across the cave's mouth.

Then dark was the Plain of High Heaven, and black dark the Central Land of Reed Plains, and eternal night prevailed. Hereupon the voices of the deities as they wandered over the face of the earth were like unto the flies in the fifth moon, and from far and near there arose portents of woe. Therefore did the Eight Hundred Myriad Deities assemble with a divine assembly in the dry bed of the Tranquil River of Heaven, there to hold parley, and to make decision what should be done. And His Augustness the Lord of Deep Thoughts commanded them. So they called together the Singing Birds of Eternal Night. And they charged Ama- tsu- mara, the Divine Smith, to make them a mirror of shining white metal. And they charged Tama- noya- no- mikoto to string together many hundreds of curved jewels. And, having performed divination by the shoulder- blade of a stag of Mount Kagu, they uprooted a sacred tree, a *sakaki*, of five hundred branches. And they hung the jewels upon the branches of the tree, and they hung the mirror upon its branches. And all the lower branches they covered with offerings, streamers of white and streamers of blue, and they bore the tree before the rock cavern where the Sun Goddess was. And immediately the assembled birds sang. Then a divine maiden of fair renown, who for grace and skill in dancing had no sister, either in the Land of Rice Ears or upon the Plain of High Heaven, stood before the cavern door. And there was hung about her for a garland the club moss from Mount Kagu, and her head was bound with the leaves of the spindle- tree and with flowers of gold and flowers of silver, and a sheaf of green bamboo- grass was in her hands. And she danced before the cavern door as one possessed, for heaven and earth have not seen the like of her dancing. It was more lovely than the pine- tops waving in the wind or the floating of sea foam, and the cloud race upon the Plain of High Heaven is not to be compared with it. And the earth quaked and High Heaven shook, and all the Eight Hundred Myriad Deities laughed together.

Now Ama Terassu, the Glory of Heaven, lay in the rock cavern, and the bright light streamed from her fair body in rays, so that she was as a great jewel of price. And pools of water gleamed in the floor of the cavern, and the slime upon the walls gleamed with many colours, and the small rock- plants flourished in the unwonted heat, so that the heavenly lady lay in a bower and slept. And she awoke because of the song of the Eternal Singing Birds, and she raised herself and flung the hair back over her shoulder, and said, "Alack, the poor birds that sing in the long night!" And there came to her the sound of dancing and of high revel and of the merriment of the gods, so she was still and listened. And presently she felt the Plain of High Heaven shake, and heard the Eight Hundred Myriad Deities as they laughed together. And she arose and came to the door of the cavern, and rolled back the great stone a little way. And a beam of light fell upon the dancing maiden where she stood, panting, in all her array; but the other deities were yet in darkness, and they looked at each other and were still. Then spoke the Fair Glory of Heaven: "Methought that because I was hidden the Plain of High Heaven should be dark, and black dark the Central Land of Reed Plains. How, then, doth the Dancing Maiden go thus, adorned with garlands and her head tired? And why do the Eight Hundred Myriad Deities laugh together?"

Then the Dancing Maiden made answer: "O Thine Augustness, that art the sweet delight of all the deities, behold the divine maidens are decked with flowers, and the gods assemble with shouts. We rejoice and are glad because there is a goddess more illustrious than Thine Augustness."

And Ama Terassu heard and was wroth. And she covered her face with her long sleeves, so that the deities should not see her tears; howbeit, they fell like the falling stars. Then the youths of the Court of Heaven stood by the *sakaki* tree, where hung the mirror that was made by Ama- tsu- Mara, the Divine Smith. And they cried, "Lady, look and behold the new paragon of Heaven!"

And Ama Terassu said, "Indeed, I will not behold." Nevertheless, she presently let slip the sleeves that covered her countenance and looked in the mirror. And as she looked, and beheld, and was dazzled by her own beauty, that was without peer, she came forth slowly from the rocks of the cavern. And the light of her flooded High Heaven, and below the rice ears waved and shook themselves, and the wild cherry rushed into flower. And all the deities joined their hands in a ring about Ama Terassu, the Goddess of the Sun, and the door of the rock cavern was shut. Then the Dancing Maiden cried, "O Lady, Thine

Augustness, how should any Deity be born to compare with thee, the Glory of Heaven?"

So with joy they bore the goddess to her place.

But Susa, the Swift, the Brave, the Impetuous, the Long- Haired, the Thrice Unhappy, the Lord of the Sea, him the deities arraigned to stand trial in the dry bed of the Tranquil River of Heaven. And they took counsel, and fined him with a great fine. And, having shorn him of his hair, which was his beauty and his pride (for it was blue- black as an iris, and hung below his knee), they banished him for ever from the heavenly precincts.

So Susa descended to earth by the Floating Bridge with bitterness in his heart, and for many days he wandered in despair, he knew not whither. By fair rice- fields he came, and by barren moors, heeding nothing; and at last he stayed to rest by the side of the river called Hi, which is in the land of Izumo.

And as he sat, moody, his head on his hand, and looked down at the water, he beheld a chopstick floating on the surface of the stream. So Susa, the Impetuous, arose immediately, saying, "There are people at the river head." And he pursued his way up the bank in quest of them. And when he had gone not a great way, he found an old man weeping and lamenting very grievously, among the reeds and willows by the water-side. And there was with him a lady of great state and beauty, like unto the daughter of a deity; but her fair eyes were marred with many tears, and she moaned continually and wrung her hands. And these twain had between them a young maid of very slender and delicate form; but her face Susa could not see, for she covered it with a veil. And ever and anon she moved and trembled with fear, or seemed to beseech the old man earnestly, or plucked the lady by the sleeve; at which these last but shook their heads sorrowfully, and returned to their lamentations.

And Susa, full of wonder, drew near and asked the old man, "Who art thou?"

And the old man answered, "I am an earthly deity of the mountains. This is my wife, who weeps with me by the water-side, and the child is my youngest daughter."

And Susa inquired of him again, "What is the cause of your weeping and lamentation?"

And he answered, "Know, sir, that I am an earthly deity of renown, and I was the father of eight fair daughters. But a horror broods over the land, for every year at this time it is ravaged by a monster, the eight-forked serpent of Koshi, that delights in the flesh of young virgins. In seven years have my seven sweet children been devoured. And now the time of my youngest- born is at hand. Therefore do we weep, O Thine Augustness."

Then said Susa, the Impetuous, "What is the likeness of this monster?"

And the deities of the mountain made answer: "His eyes are fiery and red as the *akakagachi* (that is, the winter cherry). He has but one body, with eight heads and eight scaly tails. Moreover, on his body grows moss, together with the fir and the cryptomeria of the forest. In his going he covers eight valleys and eight hills, and upon his under side he is red and gory."

Then the Lord Susa, the Impetuous, cried, "My lord, give me thy daughter."

And the earthly deity, seeing his strength and great beauty and the brightness of his countenance, knew that he was a god, and answered, "With all reverence do I offer her unto thee. Howbeit, I know not thine august name."

And Susa said, "I am Susa, the Sea God, the exile of High Heaven."

And the mountain deity and also his fair wife spoke, saying, "So be it, Thine Augustness, take the young maid."

And immediately Susa flung away the veil and saw the face of his bride, pale as the moon in winter. And he touched her on the forehead, and said, "Fair and beloved, fair and beloved...."

And the maid flushed faintly to stand thus barefaced. Howbeit, she had little need, for the tears that stood in my lord Susa's eyes were veil enough for her modesty. And he said again, "Dear and beautiful, our pleasure shall be hereafter, now we may not tarry."

So he took the young maid at once, and changed her into a crown for his head. And Susa wore the crown gallantly. And he instructed the earthly deity, and together they brewed *saké*, refined eight- fold; and with the *saké* they filled eight vats and set them in readiness; and when all was prepared they waited. And presently there was a mighty noise, like the sound of an earthquake, and the hills and valleys shook. And the serpent crawled in sight, huge and horrible, so that the earthly deities hid their faces for fear. But Susa, the Impetuous, gazed upon the serpent with his sword drawn.

Now the serpent had eight heads, and immediately he dipped a head into each vat of *saké* and drank long. Thereupon he became drunken with the distilled liquor, and all the heads lay down and slept.

Then the Lord Susa brandished his ten-grasp sword, and leapt upon the monster and cut off the eight heads with eight valiant strokes. So the serpent was slain with a great slaying, and the river Hi flowed on, a river of blood. And Susa cut the tails of the serpent also, and as he struck the fourth tail the edge of his august sword was turned back. So he probed with its point, and found a great jewelled sword with a blade sharp as no known smith could temper it. And he took the sword and sent it for an offering to the Sun Goddess, his august sister. This is the herb- quelling sword.

And Susa, the Impetuous, built him a palace at the place called Suga, and dwelt there with his bride. And the clouds of heaven hung like a curtain round about the palace. Then the Lord Susa sang this song:

"Many clouds arise. The manifold fence of the forth-issuing clouds Makes a manifold fence, For the spouses to be within. Oh, the manifold fence...."

The Wind in the Pine Tree

It was a Deity from High Heaven that planted the Pine Tree.

So long ago that the crane cannot remember it, and the tortoise knows it only by hearsay from his great- grandmother, the heavenly deity descended. Lightly, lightly he came by way of the Floating Bridge, bearing the tree in his right hand. Lightly, lightly his feet touched the earth.

He said, "I have come to the Land of the Reed Plains. I have come to the Land of Fresh Rice Ears. It is a good land; I am satisfied." And he planted the Pine Tree within the sound of the sea at Takasaga, which is in the Province of Harima. Then he went up again to High Heaven by way of the Floating Bridge.

But the Pine Tree flourished. So great it grew, there was not a greater in all the Land of the Reed Plains. Its trunk was rosy red, and beneath it spread a brown carpet of fallen needles.

In the sweet nights of summer the Children of the Woods came hand in hand to the Pine Tree by moonlight, slipping their slim dark feet upon the moss, and tossing back their long green hair.

The Children of the Water came by moonlight, all drenching wet their sleeves, and the bright drops fell from their finger- tips. The Children of the Air rested in the Pine Tree's branches, and made murmuring music all the live- long night. The Children of the Sea Foam crept up the yellow sands; and from the confines of Yomi came the Mysteries, the Sounds and the Scents of the Dark- with faces veiled and thin grey forms, they came, and they hung upon the air about the place where the Pine Tree was, so that the place was holy and haunted.

Lovers wandering upon the beach at Takasaga would hear the great company of Spirits singing together.

"Joy of my heart," they said to one another, "do you hear the wind in the Pine Tree?"

Poor souls lying sick a- bed would listen, and fishermen far out at sea would pause in their labour to whisper, "The wind, the wind in the Pine Tree! How the sound carries over the water!"

As for the coming of the Maiden, the crane cannot remember it, but the tortoise has it of his great- grandmother that she was born of poor parents in Takasaga. The Maiden was brown and tall and slender; in face and form most lovely. Her hair hung down to her knees. She rose at dawn to help her mother; she found sticks for the fire, she drew water at the well. She could spin and weave with the best; and for long, long hours she sat and plied her wheel or her shuttle in the shade of the great Pine Tree, whilst her ears heard the sound of the wind in its branches. Sometimes her eyes looked out over the paths of the sea, as one who waits and watches. She was calm, not restless, more grave than gay, though she smiled not seldom. Her voice was the voice of a Heavenly Being.

Now concerning the Youth from the far province, of him the crane knows something, for the crane is a great traveller. She was flying over the streams and the valleys of the far province, so she says, when she saw the Youth at work in the green rice- fields. The crane lingered, circling slowly in the bright air. The Youth stood up. He looked round upon the valleys and streams; he looked into the sky.

"I hear the call," he said. "I may tarry no longer. Voice in my heart, I hear and I obey."

With that he left the rice- field, and bade farewell to his mother and his father and his sisters and his brothers and his friends. All together, they came down to the seashore, weeping and clinging to each other. The

Youth took a boat and went away to sea, and the rest of them stood upon the beach.

On sped the boat for many a day over the unknown paths of the sea. And the white crane flew behind the boat. And when the wind failed, she pushed the boat forward with the wind of her strong wings.

At last, one evening about the hour of sunset, the Youth heard the sound of sweet singing. The sound came to him from the land, and it travelled over the paths of the sea. He stood up in his boat, and the crane beat her strong white wings and guided his boat to the shore till its keel touched the yellow sand of the sea- beach of Takasaga.

When the Youth had come ashore he pushed the boat out again with the waves, and watched it drift away. Then he turned his face inland. The sound of music was still in his ears. The voice was like the voice of a Heavenly Being, and strange and mystical were the words of the song:-

"The lover brought a love gift to his mistress, Jewels of jade upon a silken string; Well- carved jewels, Well-rounded jewels, Green as the grass,Upon a silken string. The jewels know not one another, The string they know, Oh, the strength of the silken string!"

The Youth went inland and came to the great Pine Tree and to the Maid that sat beneath, weaving diligently and singing. The crane came flying with her strong white wings, and perched upon the Tree's topmost branches. The tortoise lay below on the brown carpet of needles. He watched and saw much with his little eyes, but he said nothing, being very silent by nature.

The Youth stood before the Maiden, waiting.

"Whence come you?" she said, lifting up her eyes.

"I have come across the sea path. I have come from afar."

"And wherefore came you?"

"That you must know best, seeing it was your voice that sang in my heart."

"Do you bring me the gift?" she said.

"Indeed, I bring you the complete gift, jewels of jade upon a silken string."

"Come," she said, and rose and took him by the hand. And they went to her father's house.

So they drank the "Three Times Three," and were made man and wife, and lived in sweet tranquillity many, many years.

All the time the crane dwelt in the Pine Tree's topmost branches, and the tortoise on the brown carpet of needles below.

At last the Youth and Maiden, that once were, became white-haired, old, and withered, by the swift, relentless passage of years.

"Fair love," said the old man, "how weary I grow! It is sad to be old."

"Say not so, dear delight of my heart," said the old woman; "say not so, the best of all is to come."

"My dear," said the old man, "I have a desire to see the great Pine Tree before I die, and to listen once more to the song of the wind in its branches."

"Come, then," she said, and rose and took him by the hand.

Old and faint and worn, with feeble, tottering steps, and hand in hand they came.

"How faint I grow," said the old man. "Ah, I am afraid! How dark it is! Hold you my hand...."

"I have it fast in mine. There, lie down, lie down, dear love; be still and listen to the wind in the Pine Tree."

He lay on the soft brown bed beneath the Pine Tree's boughs; and the wind sang.

She who was his love and his wife bent over him and sheltered him. And he suffered the great change.

Then he opened his eyes and looked at her. She was tall and straight and slender, in face and form most lovely, and each of them was young as the gods are young. He put out his hand and touched her. "Your long black hair ..." he said.

Once more she bade him, "Come." Lightly they left the ground. To the sound of the wind's music they swayed, they floated, they rose into the air. Higher they rose and higher. The branches of the Pine Tree received them, and they were no more seen.

Still, in the sweet nights of summer, the Children of the Woods come hand in hand to the Pine Tree by moonlight, slipping their slim dark feet upon the moss, and tossing back their long green hair.

The Children of the Water come by moonlight, all drenching wet their sleeves, and the bright drops fall from their finger- tips. The Children of the Air rest in the Pine Tree's branches, and make murmuring music all the live- long night. The Children of the Sea Foam creep up the yellow sands; and from the confines of Yomi come the Mysteries, the Sounds and the Scents of the Dark- with faces veiled and thin grey forms, they come, and they hang upon the air about the place where the Pine Tree is, so that the place is holy and haunted.

Lovers wandering upon the beach at Takasaga hear the great company of Spirits singing together.

"Joy of my heart," they say to one another, "do you hear the wind in the Pine Tree?"

Flower of the Peony

Aya, sweet maid, was the only child of a *daimyo* of the Province of Omi. Mother had she none, and her father was a noble lord and a warrior. He was at the Court of the Shogun, or he had weighty affairs at the capital, or he went here and there with armies and overcame his enemies. Aya saw little of him.

Long years she dwelt with her nurse and her maidens within the walls of her father's castle. High walls were they and well- guarded, and at their foot was a deep moat which was rosy with lotus flowers all the seventh month.

When the Lady Aya was some sixteen years old her father the *daimyo* came home victorious from a foray, and she went with her maidens to meet him in the gate. She was dressed in her bravest, and as became her rank.

"My lord and father," she said, "sweet is your honourable return."

"Child, how you have grown!" her father said, astonished. "How old are you, Aya?"

"Sixteen years old, lord," she said.

"By all the gods, you are become a little great young lady, and I thought you were a baby and brought you home a doll for a home- coming gift."

He laughed, but presently afterwards grew grave, and in deep thought he went into the castle.

Soon after this he began to look about him, to find a fitting husband for his daughter.

"Best it should be done now," he said, "for a wonder has come to pass, and I am at peace with every *daimyo* in the land- and it will not last."

The Lord of Ako, in Harima, had three tall sons, fine young men and warriors all.

"The eldest is over old," said the Lord of Omi. "The youngest is a boy- but what of the middle brother? It seems to me that the middle brother should do well. They say that second thoughts are best," said the Lord of Omi.

So after messengers had come and gone, the Lady Aya was betrothed to the young Lord of Ako, and there was great rejoicing in all the country- side, for all the man and the maiden had never set eyes on one another.

The Lady Aya was very glad when she saw the presents that came from her bridegroom's house. She sat with the seamstress of the castle and fingered the soft stuffs of her fine new robes. For the rest, she played with her maidens the live- long day, or took her broidery frame, plying the needle and long silken thread. It was the month of May, and very often they took the air in a garden gallery, where Aya and her maids laughed together, and sometimes they spoke of the young Lord of Ako and how brave and beautiful he was, how skilful in art and in war, and how rich. When evening came they slipped down the gallery steps and into the garden, where they went hither and thither, hand in hand, to enjoy the cool air and the sweet scent of the flowers.

One night the Lady Aya walked in the garden according to her wont. The moon rose, round and silver.

"Ah me," sighed one of the maidens, "the moon is a love- lorn lady. Look how pale and wan she goes, and even now she will hide her eyes with her long sleeve of cloud."

"You speak sooth," returned Aya, "the moon is a love- lorn lady; but have you seen her faint sister who is sadder and fairer than she?"

"Who, then, is the moon's sister?" asked all the maidens at once.

Aya said, "Come and see- come."

With that she drew them along the paths of the garden to the still pond, where were the dancing fireflies and the frogs that sang musically. Holding each other's hands, the maidens looked down into the water, and one and all they beheld the moon's sister, and they laughed softly together. While they played by the water's brim, the Lady Aya's foot slipped upon a smooth stone, and most assuredly she would have fallen into the pond. But all of a sudden a youth leapt forward out of the sweet secrecy of the night, and caught her in his arms. For a moment all the maidens beheld the glimmer of his garments. Then he was gone. Aya stood alone, trembling. Down gazed the moon, wide- eyed and sorrowful; and still more sorrowful and sweet, upwards gazed the moon's pale sister. They saw a band of silent maidens who stood in a wilderness of blossoming peony flowers, that grew to the water's edge. It was the Lady Aya who loved them and had them planted so.

Now the lady turned without a word and moved along the paths of the garden very slowly, hanging her head. When she came to the garden gallery she left all her maidens save one, and went silently to her bower.

There she was for a long space, saying nothing. She sat and traced the pattern on her robe with the point of her finger. And Sada, her maiden, was over against her.

At length, "He was a great lord," said Aya.

"Truth, lady."

"He was young."

"He was passing well- favoured."

"Alas! he saved my life, and I had not time to thank him."

"The moon shone upon the jewelled mounting of his sword."

"And his robe that was broidered with peony flowers- my peony flowers."

"Lady, the hour grows very late."

"Well, then, untie my girdle."

"You look pale, lady."

"Small marvel, I am weary."

"Lady, what of the young Lord of Ako?"

"What of him? Why, I have not seen him. Enough, let be- no more of him. Alas! I am drowsy, I know not what I say."

After this night the Lady Aya, that had been so fresh and fair and dancing gay as a wave of the sea, fell into a pale melancholy. By day she sighed, and by night she wept. She smiled no more as she beheld her rich wedding-garments, and she would not play any more with her maidens upon the garden gallery. She wandered like a shadow, or lay speechless in her bower. And all the wise men and all the wise women of that country- side were not able to heal her of her sickness.

Then the maid Sada, weeping and hiding her face with her sleeve, went to the Lord of the House and told him of the moonlight adventure and the fair youth of the peony bed.

"Ah me," she said, "my sweet mistress pines and dies for the love of this beautiful young man."

"Child," said the *daimyo*, "how you talk! My daughter's garden is well guarded by walls and by men- at- arms. It is not possible that any stranger should enter it. What, then, is this tale of the moon and a *samurai* in peony garments and all manner of other foolishness, and how will such a tale sound in the ears of the Lord of Ako?"

But Sada wept and said, "My mistress will die."

"To fight in the field, to flatter at Court and to speak in Council, all these are easy," said the *daimyo*, "but preserve me from the affairs of my women, for they are too hard for me."

With that he made a search of all the castle and the castle grounds, but not a trace did he find of any stranger in hiding.

That night the Lady Aya called piteously for the cooler air, so they bore her out on to her garden gallery, where she lay in O Sada's arms. A minstrel of the household took his *biwa*, and to soothe her he made this song:

"*Music of my lute- Is it born, does it die, Is it truth or a lie? Whence, whence and where, Enchanted air? Music of my lute Is mute.*

"*Sweet scents in the night- Do they float, do they seem, Are they essence of dream, Or thus are they said The thoughts of the Dead? Sweet scents in the night Delight.*"

Now, while the minstrel sang and touched his instrument, a fair youth stood up from the rosy sea of peonies by the pond. All there saw him clearly, his bright eyes, his sword, and his dress broidered with flowers. The Lady Aya gave a wild cry and ran to the edge of the garden gallery, holding out her white arms. And immediately the vision passed away. But the minstrel took up his *biwa* once more and sang:

"*Love more strange than death- Is it longer than life, Is it hotter than strife? Strong, strong and blind, Transcending kind- Love more strange than death Or breath.*"

At this the mysterious knight of the flowers stood once again straight and tall, and his shining eyes were fixed upon the Lady Aya.

Then a gentleman of the company of the *daimyo*, who was a mighty man of war, drew his sword forthwith and leapt down amongst the peonies to do battle with the bold stranger that so gazed upon his master's daughter. And at that a cloud drew across the moon's face as if by faery, and of a sudden a great hot wind blew from the south. The lights died upon the garden gallery, the maidens held their garments together while their long gossamer sleeves floated out. All the peony bed was tossed about like a troubled sea, and the pink and white petals flew like foam. A mist, damp and over-sweet, hung upon the wind, so that all who were there grew faint and clung to one another, trembling.

When they were recovered, they found the night still and the moon undimmed. The soldier of the *daimyo's* company stood panting and white as death at the steps of the garden gallery. In his right hand he held his unstained sword, in his left a perfect peony flower.

"I have him," he shouted; "he could not escape me. I have him fast."

Aya said, "Give me the flower"; and he gave it her without a word, as one in a dream.

Then Aya went to her bower and slept with the peony upon her breast and was satisfied.

For nine days she kept the flower. The sweet colour came to her face, and the light to her eyes. She was perfectly healed of her sickness.

She set the peony in a bronze vase and it did not droop or fade, but grew larger and more lovely all the nine days.

At the end of this time the young Lord of Ako came riding in great pomp and state to claim his long- promised lady. So he and the Lady Aya were wed in the midst of much feasting and rejoicing. Howbeit, they say she made but a pale bride. And the same day the peony withered and was thrown away.

The Mallet

There were once two farmer men who were brothers. Both of them worked hard in seed- time and in harvest- time. They stood knee- deep in water to plant out the young rice, bending their backs a thousand times an hour; they wielded the sickle when the hot sun shone; when the rain poured down in torrents, there they were still at their digging or such like, huddled up in their rice- straw rain coats, for in the sweat of their brows did they eat their bread.

The elder of the two brothers was called Cho. For all he laboured so hard he was passing rich. From a boy he had had a saving way with him, and had put by a mint of money. He had a big farm, too, and not a year but that he did well, what with his rice, and his silk- worms, and his granaries and storehouses. But there was nothing to show for all this, if it will be believed. He was a mean, sour man with not so much as a "good day" and a cup of tea for a wayfarer, or a cake of cold rice for a beggar man. His children whimpered when he came near them, and his wife was much to be pitied.

The younger of the two brothers was called Kanè. For all he laboured so hard he was as poor as a church mouse. Bad was his luck, his silk-worms died, and his rice would not flourish. In spite of this he was a merry fellow, a bachelor who loved a song and an honest cup of *saké*. His roof, his pipe, his meagre supper, all these he would share, very gladly, with the first-comer. He had the nimblest tongue for a comical joke, and the kindest heart in the world. But it is a true thing, though it is a pity all the same, that a man cannot live on love and laughter, and presently Kanè was in a bad way.

"There's nothing for it," he says, "but to pocket my pride" (for he had some) "and go and see what my brother Cho will do for me, and I'm greatly mistaken if it will be much."

So he borrows some clothes from a friend for the visit, and sets off in very neat *hakama*, looking quite the gentleman, and singing a song to keep his heart up.

He sees his brother standing outside his house, and the first minute he thinks he is seeing a boggart, Cho is in such ragged gear. But presently he sings out, "You're early, Cho."

"You're early, Kanè," says Cho.

"May I come in and talk a bit?" asks Kanè.

"Yes," says Cho, "you can; but you won't find anything to eat at this time of day, nor yet to drink, so let disappointments be avoided."

"Very well," says Kanè; "as it happens, it's not food I've come for."

When they were inside the house and sitting on the mats, Cho says, "That's a fine suit of clothes you've got on you, Kanè. You must be doing well. It's not me that can afford to go about the muddy roads dressed up like a prince. Times are bad, very bad."

In spite of this not being a good beginning, Kanè plucks up his courage and laughs. And presently he says:

"Look here, brother. These are borrowed clothes, my own will hardly hold together. My rice crop was ruined, and my silk- worms are dead. I have not a *rin* to buy rice seed or new worms. I am at my wits' end, and I have come to you begging, so now you have it. For the sake of the mother that bore us both, give me a handful of seed and a few silk- worms' eggs."

At this Cho made as if he would faint with astonishment and dismay.

"Alack! Alack!" he says. "I am a poor man, a very poor man. Must I rob my wife and my miserable children?" And thus he bewailed himself and talked for half an hour.

But to make a long story short, Cho says that out of filial piety, and because of the blessed mother of them both, he must make shift to give Kanè the silk- worms' eggs and the rice. So he gets a handful of dead eggs and a handful of musty and mouldy rice. "These are no good to man or beast," says the old fox to himself, and he laughs. But to his own blood- brother he says, "Here, Kanè. It's the best silk- worms' eggs I am giving you, and the best rice of all my poor store, and I cannot afford it at all; and may the gods forgive me for robbing my poor wife and my children."

Kanè thanks his brother with all his heart for his great generosity, and bows his head to the mats three times. Then off he goes, with the silk- worms' eggs and the rice in his sleeve, skipping and jumping with joy, for he thought that his luck had turned at last. But in the muddy parts of the road he was careful to hold up his *hakama*, for they were borrowed.

When he reached home he gathered great store of green mulberry leaves. This was for the silk- worms that were going to be hatched out of the dead eggs. And he sat down and waited for the silk- worms to come. And come they did, too, and that was very strange, because the eggs were dead eggs for sure. The silk- worms were a lively lot; they ate the mulberry leaves in a twinkling, and lost no time at all, but began to wind themselves into cocoons that minute. Then Kanè was the happy man. He went out and told his good fortune to all the neighbours. This was where he made his mistake. And he found a peddlar man who did his rounds in those parts, and gave him a message to take to his brother Cho, with his compliments and respectful thanks, that the silk- worms were doing uncommonly well. This was where he made a bigger mistake. It was a pity he could not let well alone.

When Cho heard of his brother's luck he was not pleased. Pretty soon he tied on his straw sandals and was off to Kanè's farm. Kanè was out when he got there, but Cho did not care for that. He went to have a look at the silk- worms. And when he saw how they were beginning to spin themselves into cocoons, as neat as you please, he took a sharp knife and cut every one of them in two. Then he went away home, the bad man! When Kanè came to look after his silk-worms he could not help thinking they looked a bit queer. He scratches his head and he says, "It almost appears as though each of them has been cut in half. They seem dead," he says. Then out he goes and gathers a great lot of mulberry leaves. And all those half silk-worms set to and ate up the mulberry leaves, and after that there were just twice as many silk- worms spinning away as there were before. And that was very strange, because the silk- worms were dead for sure.

When Cho heard of this he goes and chops his own silk- worms in two with a sharp knife; but he gained nothing by that, for the silk-worms never moved again, but stayed as dead as dead, and his wife had to throw them away next morning.

After this Kanè sowed the rice seed that he had from his brother, and when the young rice came up as green as you please he planted it out with care, and it flourished wonderfully, and soon the rice was formed in the ear.

One day an immense flight of swallows came and settled on Kanè's rice- field.

"Arah! Arah!" Kanè shouted. He clapped his hands and beat about with a bamboo stick. So the swallows flew away. In two minutes back they came.

"Arah! Arah!" Kanè shouted, and he clapped his hands and beat about with his bamboo stick. So the swallows flew away. In two minutes back they came.

"Arah! Arah!" Kanè shouted. He clapped his hands and beat about with his bamboo stick. So the swallows flew away. In two minutes back they came.

When he had scared them away for the ninth time, Kanè takes his *tenegui* and wipes his face. "This grows into a habit," he says. But in two minutes back came the swallows for the tenth time. "Arah! Arah!" Kanè shouted, and he chased them over hill and dale, hedge and ditch, rice- field and mulberry- field, till at last they flew away from his sight, and he found himself in a mossy dell shaded by spreading pine trees. Being very tired with running he lies down his full length upon the moss, and presently falls fast asleep and snoring.

The next thing was that he dreamed. He thought he saw a troop of children come to the mossy glade, for in his dream he remembered very well where he was. The children fluttered here and there among the pine- trees' trunks. They were as pretty as flowers or butterflies. One and all of them had dancing bare feet; their hair hung down, long, loose and black; their skins were white like the plum blossom.

"For good or for evil," says Kanè to himself, "I have seen the fairies' children."

The children made an end of their dancing, and sat them upon the ground in a ring.

"Leader! Leader!" they cried. "Fetch us the mallet." Then there rose up a beautiful boy, about fourteen or fifteen years old, the eldest and the tallest there. He lifted a mossy stone quite close to Kanè's head. Underneath was a plain little mallet of white wood. The boy took it up and went and stood within the circle of children. He laughed and cried, "Now what will you have?"

"A kite, a kite," calls out one of the children.

The boy shakes the mallet, and lo and behold he shakes a kite out of it!- a great kite with a tail to it, and a good ball of twine as well.

"Now what else?" asks the boy.

"Battledore and shuttlecock for me," says a little girl.

And sure enough there they are, a battledore of the best, and twenty shuttlecocks, meetly feathered and gilded.

"Now what else?" says the boy.

"A lot of sweets."

"Greedy!" says the boy, but he shakes the mallet, and there are the sweets.

"A red crêpe frock and a brocade *obi*."

"Miss Vanity!" says the boy, but he shakes all this gravely out of the mallet.

"Books, story books."

"That's better," says the boy, and out come the books by the dozen and score, all open to show the lovely pictures.

Now, when the children had their hearts' desires, the leader put away the mallet beneath its mossy stone, and after they had played for some time they became tired; their bright attires melted away into the gloom of the wood, and their pretty voices grew distant and then were heard no more. It was very still.

Kanè awoke, good man, and found the sun set and darkness beginning to fall. There was the mossy stone right under his hand. He lifted it, and there was the mallet.

"Now," said Kanè, taking it up, "begging the pardon of the fairies' children, I'll make bold to borrow that mallet." So he took it home in his sleeve and spent a pleasant evening shaking gold pieces out of it, and *saké*, and new clothes, and farmers' tools, and musical instruments, and who knows what all!

It is not hard to believe that pretty soon he became the richest and jolliest farmer in all that country- side. Sleek and fat he grew, and his heart was bigger and kinder than ever.

But what like was Cho's heart when he got wind of all this? Ay, there's the question. Cho turned green with envy, as green as grass. "I'll have a fairy mallet, too," he says, "and be rich for nothing. Why should that idiot spendthrift Kanè have all the good fortune?" So he goes and begs rice from his brother, which his brother gives him very willingly, a good sackful. And he waits for it to ripen, quite wild with impatience. It ripens sure enough, and sure enough a flight of swallows comes and settles upon the good grain in the ear.

"Arah! Arah!" shouted Cho, clapping his hands and laughing aloud for joy. The swallows flew away, and Cho was after them. He chased them over hill and dale, hedge and ditch, rice- field and mulberry- field, till at last they flew away from his sight, and he found himself in a mossy dell shaded by spreading pine- trees. Cho looks about him.

"This should be the place," says he. So he lies down and waits with one wily eye shut and one wily eye open.

Presently who should trip into the dell but the fairies' children! Very fresh they were as they moved among the pine- tree trunks.

"Leader! Leader! Fetch us the mallet," they cried. Up stepped the leader and lifted away the mossy stone. And behold there was no mallet there!

Now the fairies' children became very angry. They stamped their little feet, and cried and rushed wildly to and fro, and were beside themselves altogether because the mallet was gone.

"See," cried the leader at last, "see this ugly old farmer man; he must have taken our mallet. Let us pull his nose for him."

With a shrill scream the fairies' children set upon Cho. They pinched him, and pulled him, and buffeted him, and set their sharp teeth in his flesh till he yelled in agony. Worst of all, they laid hold of his nose and pulled it. Long it grew, and longer. It reached his waist. It reached his feet.

Lord, how they laughed, the fairies' children! Then they scampered away like fallen leaves before the wind.

Cho sighed, and he groaned, and he cursed, and he swore, but for all that his nose was not an inch shorter. So, sad and sorry, he gathered it up in his two hands and went to Kanè's house.

"Kanè, I am very sick," says he.

"Indeed, so I see," says Kanè, "a terrible sickness; and how did you catch it?" he says. And so kind he was that he never laughed at Cho's nose, nor yet he never smiled, but there were tears in his eyes at his brother's misfortunes. Then Cho's heart melted and he told his brother all the tale, and he never kept back how mean he had been about the dead silk- worms' eggs, and about the other things that have been told of. And he asked Kanè to forgive him and to help him.

"Wait you still a minute," says Kanè.

He goes to his chest, and he brings out the mallet. And he rubs it very gently up and down Cho's long nose, and sure enough it shortened up very quickly. In two minutes it was a natural size. Cho danced for joy.

Kanè looks at him and says, "If I were you, I'd just go home and try to be different."

When Cho had gone, Kanè sat still and thought for a long time. When the moon rose that night he went out and took the mallet with him. He came to the mossy dell that was shaded with spreading pine trees, and he laid the mallet in its old place under the stone.

"I'm the last man in the world," he said, "to be unfriendly to the fairies' children."

The Bell of Dōjōji

The monk Anchin was young in years but
old in scholarship. Every day for many hours
he read the Great Books of the Good Law
and never wearied, and hard characters were
not hard to him.

The monk Anchin was young in years but
old in holiness; he kept his body under by
fastings and watchings and long prayers. He
was acquainted with the blessedness of
sublime meditations. His countenance was
white as ivory and as smooth; his eyes were
deep as a brown pool in autumn; his smile
was that of a Buddha; his voice was like an
angel's. He dwelt with a score of holy men in
a monastery of the mountains, where he
learned the mystic "Way of the Gods." He
was bound to his order by the strictest vows,
but was content, rejoicing in the shade of the
great pine trees and the sound of the running
water of the streams.

Now it happened that on a day in spring-
time, the old man, his Abbot, sent the young
monk Anchin upon an errand of mercy. And
he said, "My son, bind your sandals fast and
tie spare sandals to your girdle, take your hat
and your staff and your rosary and begging

bowl, for you have far to go, over mountain and stream, and across the great plain."

So the monk Anchin made him ready.

"My son," the Abbot said, "if any wayfarer do you a kindness, forget not to commend him to the gods for the space of nine existences."

"I will remember," said the monk, and so he set forth upon his way.

Over mountain and stream he passed, and as he went his spirit was wrapped in contemplation, and he recited the Holy Sutras aloud in a singing voice. And the Wise Birds called and twittered from branch to branch of the tall trees, the birds that are beloved of Buddha. One bird chanted the grand Scripture of the Nicheten, the Praise of the Sutra of the Lotus, of the Good Law, and the other bird called upon his Master's name, for he cried:

"O thou Compassionate Mind! O thou Compassionate Mind!"

The monk smiled. "Sweet and happy bird," he said.

And the bird answered,

"O thou Compassionate Mind!...

O thou Compassionate Mind!"

When the monk Anchin came to the great plain, the sun was high in the heavens, and all the blue and golden flowers of the plain languished in the noon- tide heat. The monk likewise became very weary, and when he beheld the Marshy Mere, where were bulrush and sedge that cooled their feet in the water, he laid him down to rest under a sycamore tree that grew by the Marshy Mere.

Over the mere and upon the farther side of it there hung a glittering haze.

Long did the monk Anchin lie; and as he lay he looked through the glittering haze, and as he looked the haze quivered and moved and grew and gathered upon the farther side of the mere. At the last it drew into a slender column of vapour, and out of the vapour there came forth a very dazzling lady. She wore a robe of green and gold, interwoven, and golden sandals on her slender feet. In her hands were jewels- in each hand one bright jewel like a star. Her hair was tied with a braid of scarlet, and she had a crown of scarlet flowers. She came, skirting the Marshy Mere. She came, gliding in and out of the bulrush and the sedge. In the silence there could be heard the rustle of her green skirt upon the green grass.

The monk Anchin stumbled to his feet and, trembling, he leaned against the sycamore tree.

Nearer and nearer came the lady, till she stood before Anchin and looked into his eyes. With the jewel that was in her right hand she touched his forehead and his lips. With the jewel that was in her left hand she touched his rice- straw hat and his staff and his rosary and his begging bowl. After this she had him safe in thrall. Then the wind blew a tress of her hair across his face, and when he felt it he gave one sob.

For the rest of his journey the monk went as a man in a dream. Once a rich traveller riding on horseback threw a silver coin into Anchin's begging bowl; once a woman gave him a piece of cake made of millet; and once a little boy knelt down and tied the fastening of his sandal that had become loose. But each time the monk passed on without a word, for he forgot to commend the souls of these compassionate ones for the space of nine existences. In the tree- tops the Wise Birds of Buddha sang for him no more, only from the thicket was heard the cry of the *Hototogisu*, the bird lovelorn and forsaken.

Nevertheless, well or ill, he performed his errand of mercy and returned to the monastery by another way.

Howbeit, sweet peace left him from the hour in which he had seen the lady of the

Marshy Mere. The Great Books of the Good Law sufficed him no longer; no more was he acquainted with the blessedness of divine meditations. His heart was hot within him; his eyes burned and his soul longed after the lady of the green and golden robe.

She had told him her name, and he murmured it in his sleep. "Kiohimé- Kiohimé!" Waking, he repeated it instead of his prayers- to the great scandal of the brethren, who whispered together and said, "Is our brother mad?"

At length Anchin went to the good Abbot, and in his ear poured forth all his tale in a passion of mingled love and grief, humbly asking what he must do.

The Abbot said, "Alack, my son, now you suffer for sin committed in a former life, for Karma must needs be worked out."

Anchin asked him, "Then is it past help?"

"Not that," said the Abbot, "but you are in a very great strait."

"Are you angry with me?" said Anchin.

"Nay, Heaven forbid, my poor son."

"Then what must I do?"

"Fast and pray, and for a penance stand in the ice- cold water of our mountain torrent an hour at sunrise and an hour at sunset. Thus shall you be purged from carnal affection and escape the perils of illusion."

So Anchin fasted and prayed, he scourged his body, and hour after hour he did penance in the ice- cold water of the torrent. Wan as a ghost he grew, and his eyes were like flames. His trouble would not leave him. A battle raged in his breast. He could not be faithful to his vows and faithful to his love.

The brethren wondered, "What can ail the monk Anchin, who was so learned and so holy- is he bewitched by a fox or a badger, or can he have a devil?"

But the Abbot said, "Let be."

Now on a hot night of summer, the monk being sleepless in his cell, he was visited by Kiohimé, the magic lady of the mere. The moonlight was on her hands and her long sleeves. Her robe was green and gold, interwoven; golden were her sandals. Her hair was braided with scarlet and adorned with scarlet flowers.

"Long, long have I waited for thee on the plains," she said. "The night wind sighs in the sedge- the frogs sing by the Marshy Mere. Come, lord...."

But he cried, "My vows that I have vowed- alas! the love that I love. I keep faith and loyalty, the bird in my bosom... I may not come."

She smiled, "*May* not?" she said, and with that she lifted the monk Anchin in her arms.

But he, gathering all his strength together, tore himself from her and fled from the place. Barefooted and bareheaded he went, his white robe flying, through the dark halls of the monastery, where the air was heavy with incense and sweet with prayers, where the golden Amida rested upon her lotus, ineffably smiling. He leaped the grey stone steps that led down from her shrine and gained the pine trees and the mountain path. Down, down he fled on the rough way, the nymph Kiohimé pursuing. As for her, her feet never touched the ground, and she spread her green sleeves like wings. Down, down they fled together, and so close was she behind him that the monk felt her breath upon his neck.

"As a young goddess, she is fleet of foot ..." he moaned.

At last they came to the famed temple of Dōjōji, which was upon the plains. By this Anchin sobbed and staggered as he ran; his knees failed him and his head swam.

"I am lost," he cried, "for a hundred existences." But with that he saw the great temple bell of Dōjōji that hung but a little way from the ground. He cast himself down and crept beneath it, and so deemed himself sheltered and secure.

Then came Kiohimé, the Merciless Lady, and the moonlight shone upon her long sleeves. She did not sigh, nor cry, nor call upon her love. She stood still for a little space and smiled. Then lightly she sprang to the top of the great bronze bell of Dōjōji, and with her sharp teeth she bit through the ropes that held it, so that the bell came to the ground and the monk was a prisoner. And Kiohimé embraced the bell with her arms. She crept about it, she crawled about it and her green robe flowed over it. Her green robe glittered with a thousand golden scales; long flames burst from her lips and from her eyes; a huge and fearsome Dragon, she wound and coiled herself about the bell of Dōjōji. With her Dragon's tail she lashed the bell, and lashed it till its bronze was red hot.

Still she lashed the bell, while the monk called piteously for mercy. And when he was very quiet she did not stop. All the night long the frogs sang by the Marshy Mere and the wind sighed in the sedges. But the Dragon Lady was upon the bell of Dōjōji, and she lashed it furiously with her tail till dawn.

The Maiden of Unai

The Maiden of Unai was fair as an earthly
deity, but the eyes of man might not behold
her. She dwelt in a hidden place in her father's
house, and of what cheer she made the live-
long day not a soul could tell, but her father
who kept watch, and her mother who kept
ward, and her ancient nurse who tended her.
The cause was this.

When the maid was about seven years old,
with her black hair loose and hanging to her
shoulder, an ancient man, a traveller, came,
footsore and weary, to her father's house. He
was made welcome, served with rice and with
tea, whilst the master of the house sat by, and
the mistress, to do him honour. Meanwhile
the little maid was here and there, catching at
her mother's sleeve, pattering with bare feet
over the mats, or bouncing a great green and
scarlet ball in a corner. And the stranger lifted
his eyes and marked the child.

After he had eaten, he called for a bowl of
clear water, and taking from his wallet a
handful of fine silver sand he let it slip
through his fingers and it sank to the bottom
of the bowl. In a little he spoke.

"My lord," he said to the master of the
house, "I was hungry and weary, and you have

fed me and refreshed me. I am a poor man and it is hard for me to show my gratitude. Now I am a soothsayer by profession, very far- famed for the skill of my divination. Therefore, in return for your kindness I have looked into the future of your child. Will you hear her destiny?"

The child knelt in a corner of the room bouncing her green and scarlet ball.

The master of the house bade the soothsayer speak on.

This one looked down into the bowl of water where the sand was, and said: "The Maiden of Unai shall grow up fairer than the children of men. Her beauty shall shine as the beauty of an earthly deity. Every man who looks upon her shall pine with love and longing, and when she is fifteen years old there shall die for her sake a mighty hero from near, and a valiant hero from afar. And there shall be sorrow and mourning because of her, loud and grievous, so that the sound of it shall reach High Heaven and offend the peace of the gods."

The master of the house said, "Is this a true divination?"

"Indeed, my lord," said the soothsayer, "it is too true." And with that he bound on his sandals, and taking his staff and his great hat of rice- straw, he spoke no other word, but went his ways; neither was he any more seen nor heard tell of upon that country- side.

And the child knelt in a corner of the room, bouncing her green and scarlet ball.

The father and mother took counsel.

The mother wept, but she said, "Let be, for who can alter the pattern set up upon the looms of the weaving women of Heaven?" But the father cried, "I will fight. I will avert the portent; the thing shall not come to pass. Who am I that I should give credence to a dog of a soothsayer who lies in his teeth?" And though his wife shook her head and moaned, he gave her counsel no heed, for he was a man.

So they hid the child in a secret chamber, where an old wise woman tended her, fed her, bathed her, combed her hair, taught her to make songs and to sing, to dance so that her feet moved like rosy butterflies over the white mats, or to sit at a frame with a wonder of needlework stretched upon it, drawing the needle and the silken thread hour after hour.

For eight years the maid set eyes upon no human being save her father, her mother, and her nurse, these three only. All the day she spent in her distant chamber, far removed from the sights and the sounds of the world.

Only in the night she came forth into her father's garden, when the moon shone and the birds slept and the flowers had no colour. And with every season that passed the maid grew more beautiful. Her hair hung down to her knees and was black as a thundercloud. Her forehead was the plum blossom, her cheek the wild cherry, and her mouth the flower of the pomegranate. At fifteen years old she was the loveliest thing that ever saw the light, and the sun was sick with jealousy because only the moon might shine upon her.

In spite of all, the fame of her beauty became known, and because she was kept so guarded men thought of her the more, and because she might not be seen men longed to behold her. And because of the mystery and the maiden, gallants and warriors and men of note came from far and near and flocked to the house of Unai; and they made a hedge about it with themselves and their bright swords; and they swore that they would not leave the place till they had sight of the maid, and this they would have either by favour or by force.

Then the master of the house did even as he must, and he sent her mother to bring the maid down. So the mother went, taking with her a robe of grey silk and a great girdle of brocade, green and gold; and she found the maid, her daughter, sitting in her secret chamber singing.

The maid sang thus:

"Nothing has changed since the time of the gods, Neither the running of water nor the way of love."

And the mother was astonished and said, "What manner of song is this, and where heard you of such a thing as love?"

And she answered, "I have read of it in a book."

Then they took her, her mother and the wise woman, and they tied her hair and pinned it high upon her head with gold and coral pins, and held it with a great lacquer comb. She said, "How heavy it is!"

While they dressed her in the robe of grey silk, and tied the girdle of brocade, first she shuddered and said, "I am cold." Then they would have thrown over her a mantle broidered with plum blossom and pine, but she would have none of it, saying, "No, no, I burn."

They painted her lips with *beni*, and when she saw it she murmured, "Alack, there is blood upon my lips!" But they led her down and out on to a balcony, where the men who were assembled might see her. She was fairer than the children of men, and her beauty shone like the beauty of an earthly deity. And all the warriors who were there looked upon her and were silent, for already they were faint with love and longing. And the maid stood with eyes cast down, and slowly the hot blush rose to her cheek and she was lovelier than before.

Three or four score men of name sought her hand, being distraught for love of her, and amongst them were two braver and nobler than the rest. The one came from afar and was the champion of Chinu, and the other came from near, the champion of Unai. They were young, strong, and black- haired. They were equal in years, in strength, and in valour. Both were girded with great swords, and full-charged quivers were upon their backs, and six- foot bows of white wood were in their hands. Together they stood beneath the balcony of the maiden of Unai, like twin brothers in beauty and attainments. Together they cried aloud with passionate voices, telling of their eternal love, and bidding the maiden choose between them.

She lifted up her eyes and looked fixedly upon them, but spoke no word.

Then they drew their swords and made as if to fight the matter out there and then; but the maid's father spoke: "Put up your swords, fair sirs; I have devised a better way for the decision of this thing. If it please you, enter my house."

Now part of the house of Unai was built out upon a platform over the river that flowed past. It was the fifth month and the wistaria was in blossom upon the trellis, and hung downwards nearly into the water. The river was swift and deep. Here the master of the house brought the champions, and the maiden was there also. But the mother and the wise woman stood a little way apart, and hid their faces in their long sleeves. Presently a white water- bird dropped from the blue sky, and rocked to and fro upon the water of the river.

"Now, champions," cried the father of the maiden, "draw me your bows and let fly each of you an arrow at yonder white bird that floats upon the river. He that shall strike the bird and prove himself to be the better marksman, he shall wed my daughter, the peerless Maiden of Unai."

Then immediately the two champions drew their bows of white wood and let fly each of them an arrow. Each arrow sped swift; each arrow struck true. The champion of Chinu struck the water- bird in the head, but the champion of Unai struck her in the tail so that the white feathers were scattered. Then the champions cried, "Enough of this trifling. There is but one way." And again their bright swords leapt from their scabbards.

But the maid stood trembling, holding the gnarled stem of the wistaria in her hands. She trembled and shook the branches so that the frail flowers fell about her. "My lords, my lords," she cried, "oh, brave and beautiful heroes of fame, it is not meet that one of you should die for such as I am. I honour you; I love you both- therefore farewell." With that, still holding to the wistaria, she swung herself clear of the balcony and dropped into the deep and swift- flowing river. "Weep not," she cried, "for no woman dies to- day. It is but a child that is lost." And so she sank.

Down sprang the champion of Chinu into the flood, and in the same instant down sprang the champion of Unai. Alack, they were heavy with the arms that they bore, and they sank and were entangled in the long water weeds. And so the three of them were drowned.

But at night when the moon shone, the pale dead rose, floating to the surface of the water. The champion of Unai held the maiden's right hand in his own, but the champion of Chinu lay with his head against the maiden's heart, bound close to her by a tress of her long hair; and as he lay he smiled.

The three corpses they lifted from the water, and laid them together upon a bier of fair white wood, and over them they strewed herbs and sweet flowers, and laid a veil over their faces of fine white silk. And they lighted fires and burned incense. Gallants and warriors and men of note who loved the maiden, alive or dead, stood about her bier and made a hedge with themselves and their bright swords. And there was sorrow and mourning, loud and grievous, so that the sound of it reached High Heaven and offended the peace of the gods.

A grave was dug wide and deep, and the three were buried therein. The maid they laid in the middle, and the two champions upon either side. Idzumo was the native place of the champion of Chinu, so they brought earth from thence in a junk, and with this earth they covered him.

So the maid slept there in the grave, the champions faithfully guarding her, for they had buried with them their bows of white wood and their good armour and their spears and their bright swords. Nothing was forgotten that is needful for adventure in the Land of Yomi.

The Robe of Feathers

Mio Strand is in the Province of Suruga. Its sand is yellow and fine, strewn with rose shells at the ebb tide. Its pine trees are ancient and they lean all one way, which is the way that the wild wind wills. Before Mio rolls the deep sea, and behind Mio rises Fugi, the most sacred, the mountain of mountains. Small marvel that the Strange People should come to Mio.

Of the Strange People not much is known, even at Mio, though it is sure they come there. It seems they are shy indeed, more's the pity. They come through the blue air, or across the mysterious paths of the sea. Their footprints are never, never seen upon the wet beach, for they tread too lightly. But sometimes in their dancing they sweep their robes upon the sand and leave it ribbed and ruffled; so, often enough, it may be seen at Mio.

This is not all. Once a fisherman of Mio set eyes upon a maiden of the Strange People, and talked with her and made her do his bidding. This is a true thing, and thus it came about.

The fisherman was out in his boat all night. He cast his net here and he cast his net there, but he caught nothing at all for his pains. It may be believed that he grew weary enough before the morning. In the cold of the dawn he brought his boat to shore and set foot on Mio Strand, shivering.

Then, so he says, a warm wind met him and blew through his garments and his hair, so that he flushed and glowed. The very sand was full of comfort to his chilly feet. Upon the warm wind a fragrance was borne, cedar and vervain, and the scent of a hundred flowers.

Flowers dropped softly through the air like bright rain. The fisherman stretched out his hands and caught them, lotus and jessamine and pomegranate. And all the while sweet music sounded.

"This is never Mio Strand," cried the fisherman, bewildered, "where I have pulled my boat ashore a thousand times or flown kites upon a holiday. Alack, I fear me I have sailed to the Fortunate Isles unawares, or come unwilling to the Sea King's garden; or very like I am dead and never knew it, and this is Yomi. O Yomi, Land of Yomi, how like thou art to Mio Strand, my dear home!"

After he had said this, the fisherman looked up the beach and down the beach, and he turned and saw Fuji, the mountain of mountains, and then he turned and saw the deep rolling sea and knew he was at Mio and no other place, and gave a long sigh.

"Thanks be," he said, and lifting his eyes he saw a robe of feathers hanging upon the branch of a pine tree. In the robe were feathers of all the birds that fly, every one; the kingfisher and the golden pheasant, the love bird, the swan, the crow, the cormorant, the dove, the bullfinch, the falcon, the plover, and the heron.

"Ah, the pretty fluttering thing!" said the fisherman, and he took it from the pine tree where it hung.

"Ah, the warm, sweet, fairy thing!" said the fisherman; "I'll take it home for a treasure, sure no money could buy it, and I'll show it to all the folk of the village." And off he set for home with the fairy feathers over his arm.

Now the maiden of the Strange People had been playing all this time with the White Children of the Foam that live in the salt sea. She looked up through the cold clear water and marked that her robe hung no longer on the pine- tree branch.

"Alas, alas!" she cried, "my robe, my feather robe!" Swifter than any arrow she sprang from the water, and sped, fleet of foot, along the wet sand. The White Children of the Foam followed at her flashing heels. Clad in the cloak of her long hair, she came up with the fisherman.

"Give me my feather robe," she said, and held out her hand for it.

"Why?" said the fisherman.

"'Tis mine. I want it. I must have it."

"Oho," said the fisherman, "finding's keeping," and he didn't give her the feather robe.

"I am a Fairy," she said.

"Farewell, Fairy," said the fisherman.

"A Moon Fairy," she said.

"Farewell, Moon Fairy," said the fisherman, and he made to take his way along Mio Strand. At that she snatched at the feather robe, but the fisherman held fast. The feathers fluttered out and dropped upon the sand.

"I wouldn't do that," said the fisherman. "You'll have it all to pieces."

"I am a Moon Fairy, and at dawn I came to play upon fair Mio Strand; without my feathers I cannot go back to my place, my home in High Heaven. Therefore give me my feathers."

"No," said the fisherman.

"Oh, fisherman, fisherman, give me my robe."

"I couldn't think of it," said the fisherman.

At this the maiden fell upon her knees and drooped like a lily in the heat of the day. With her arms she held the fisherman about the knees, and as she clung to him beseeching him, he felt her tears upon his bare feet.

She wept and said:

"*I am a bird, a frail bird, A wounded bird with broken wings, I must die far from home, For the Five Woes are come upon me. The red flowers in my hair are faded; My robe is made unclean; Faintness comes upon me; I cannot see- farewell, dear sight of my eyes; I have lost joy. Oh, blessed flying clouds, and happy birds, And golden dust in the wind, And flying thoughts and flying prayers! I have lost all joy.*"

"Oh, stop," said the fisherman, "you may have your robe."

"Give," she cried.

"Softly, softly," said the fisherman. "Not so fast. I will give you your robe if you will dance for me here on Mio Strand."

"What must I dance?" she asked.

"You must dance the mystic dance that makes the Palace of the Moon turn round."

She said, "Give me my feathers and I will dance it. I cannot dance without my feathers."

"What if you cheat me, what if you break your promise and fly immediately to the moon and no dancing at all?"

"Ah, fisherman," she said, "the faith of a Fairy!"

Then he gave her the robe.

Now, when she had arrayed herself and flung back her hair, the Fairy began to dance upon the yellow sand. In and out of the feather robe crept her fairy feet. Slowly, softly, she went with folded wings and sang:

"Oh, the gold and silver mountains of the Moon, And the sweet Singing Birds of Heaven! They sing in the branches of the cinnamon tree, To entertain the thirty kings that are there. Fifteen kings in white garments, To reign for fifteen days. Fifteen kings in black garments, To reign for fifteen days. I hear the music of Heaven; Away, away, I fly to Fairy Places."

At this the Fairy spread her rainbow-coloured wings, and the wind that they made fluttered the red flowers in her hair. Out streamed the robe of feathers bright and gay.

The Fairy laughed. Her feet touched the waves of the sea; her feet touched the grass and the flowers inshore. They touched the high branches of the pines and then the white clouds.

"Farewell, fisherman!" the Fairy cried, and he saw her no more.

Long, long he stood gazing up into the sky. At length he stooped and picked up a little feather from the shore, a grey dove's feather.

He smoothed it out with his finger and hid it in his girdle.

Then he went to his home.

The Singing Bird of Heaven

Ama Terassu, the Glorious, the Light of High Heaven, commanded, saying, "His Augustness, my August Child, who is called the Conqueror, shall descend to the land. For it is a Land of Luxuriant Reed Plains, a Land of Fresh Rice Ears, a Land of a Thousand Autumns. So of this land he shall be king."

Now his Augustness, the August Child, the Conqueror, stood upon the Floating Bridge of Heaven and looked down, and he saw that there was a great unquietness upon the Land of the Reed Plains. For earthly deities made strife, and blood ran, and fearful sounds of war arose, even to High Heaven. So the August Child, the heavenly born, turned back across the Floating Bridge, and swore he would not descend to rule the land until it should be cleansed.

And Ama Terassu, the Light of High Heaven, who had the sun set fast between her eyes, bound her head with jewels, and gathered the deities together in a divine assembly, to hold council in the Tranquil River Bed. And she spoke and said, "Who shall subdue the land that I have given to the August Child?"

And all the deities cried, "O Thine Augustness, send down the Lord of Spears." Therefore the Lord of Spears went lightly down by the Floating Bridge; and there were bound upon his back eight hundred spears. Howbeit, he made a truce with the Lord of the Reed Plains and tarried there; and for three years there was no report.

Therefore, once more the Queen of Heaven called him whom the gods name Wonderful, and she called the Lord of Deep Thoughts, and likewise she called every deity of Heaven, and they came to council in the Tranquil River Bed, so that upon the sand there was left the print of their august feet. And Ama Terassu said, "Behold now the Lord of Spears is faithless. Whom shall we send to rule the land?" And the Young Prince answered, "O Mother of Heaven, Thine Augustness, send me." And all the deities assented with one accord and cried, "Send him, send him," till there was a sound like thunder in the River Bed.

So the Young Prince bound on his sandals, and they brought to him the great bow that stands in the Hall of High Heaven, and bestowed it upon him, and they gave him many heavenly- feathered arrows. So they made him ready, and they brought him to the

Floating Bridge. And the Young Prince descended lightly, while his garments shone with the glory of Heaven. But when he touched the tops of the high hills, his heart beat fast and his blood ran warm. Therefore he cut the fastening of his sandals and cast them behind him, and he ran upon his bare feet, like an earthly deity, and came to the palace upon the Reed Plains.

Now, at the door of the palace the Princess Undershining stood, like a growing flower. So the Young Prince beheld her and loved her, and he built him a dwelling upon the Reed Plains, and took the Princess for his bride. And, because he loved her and her earthly children, he brought no report to High Heaven, and he forgot the waiting deities. For Heaven was vague to him as a dream.

But the gods were weary.

And Ama Terassu said, "Long, long tarries our messenger, and brings no word again. My Lord, the August Child, waxes impatient; whom now shall we send?" Thereupon, all the deities, and the Lord of Deep Thoughts, replied, "Send down the Singing Bird, the beloved of High Heaven."

So Ama Terassu took the golden Singing Bird, and said, "Sweet music of the divine gods, spread thou thy bright wings, and fly to the Land of Reed Plains, and there search out the Young Prince, the messenger of Heaven, and, when thou hast found him, sing in his ear this song: 'Ama Terassu, the Goddess of the Sun, has sent me saying, How fares the quest of High Heaven, and how fares the message? Where is the report of the gods?'"

So the bird departed, singing. And she came to the Land of the Reed Plains, and perched upon the branch of a fair cassia tree which grew hard by the Young Prince's dwelling. Day and night, she sang, and the gods in Heaven thought long for their sweet Singing Bird. Howbeit she returned not again, but sat upon the branch of the cassia tree.

But the Young Prince gave no heed.

And She that Speaketh Evil heard the words that the bird sang. And she whispered in the Young Prince's ear, "See now, my lord, this is an evil bird, and evil is its cry; therefore take thou thine arrows and go forth and slay it." So she urged continually, and, by glamour, she prevailed upon him. Then the Young Prince arose, and took his bow and his heavenly-feathered arrows, and he let fly an arrow into the branches of the cassia tree. And suddenly the sweet sound of singing ceased, and the golden bird fell dead, for the aim was true.

But the heavenly- feathered arrow took wing and pierced the floor of Heaven, and reached the high place, where sat the Sun Goddess, together with her August Counsellors, in the Tranquil River Bed of Heaven. And the god called Wonderful took up the arrow, and beheld the blood upon its feathers. And the Lord of Deep Thoughts said, "This is the arrow that was given to the Young Prince," and he showed it to all the deities. And he said, "If the Young Prince has shot this arrow at the evil deities, according to our command, let it do him no hurt. But, if his heart be not pure, then let the Young Prince perish by this arrow." And he hurled the arrow back to earth.

Now the Young Prince lay upon a couch, sleeping. And the arrow fell, and pierced his heart that he died.

Yet the sweet Singing Bird of Heaven returned no more; and the gods were sorrowful.

Howbeit, the Young Prince lay dead upon his bed; and the wailing of his spouse, the Princess Undershining, re- echoed in the wind, and was heard in Heaven. So the Young Prince's father descended with cries and lamentations, and there was built a mourning house upon the Land of Reed Plains, and the Young Prince was laid there.

And there came to mourn for him the wild goose of the river, and the pheasant, and the kingfisher. And they mourned for him eight days and eight nights.

The Cold Lady

Once an old man and a young man left their village in company, in order to make a journey into a distant province. Now, whether they went for pleasure or for profit, for matters of money, of love or war, or because of some small or great vow that they had laid upon their souls, it is no longer known. All these things were very long since forgotten. It is enough to say that it is likely they accomplished their desires, for they turned their faces homewards about the setting- in of the winter season, which is an evil time for wayfarers, Heaven knows.

Now as they journeyed, it happened that they missed their way, and, being in a lonely part of the country, they wandered all the day long and came upon no good soul to guide them. Near nightfall they found themselves upon the brink of a broad and swift- flowing river. There was no bridge, no ford, no ferry. Down came the night, with pitch- black clouds and a little shrewd wind that blew the dry and scanty reeds. Presently the snow came. The flakes fell upon the dark water of the river.

"How white, how white they are!" cried the young man.

But the old man shivered. In truth it was bitter cold, and they were in a bad case. Tired out, the old man sat him down upon the ground; he drew his cloak round him and clasped his hands about his knees. The young man blew upon his fingers to warm them. He went up the bank a little, and at last he found a small poor hut, deserted by a charcoal-burner or ferryman.

"Bad it is at the best," said the young man, "yet the gods be praised for any shelter on such a night." So he carried his companion to the hut. They had no food and no fire, but there was a bundle of dried leaves in the corner. Here they lay down and covered themselves with their straw rain- coats; and in spite of the cold, they soon fell asleep.

About midnight the young man was awakened by an icy air upon his cheek. The door of the hut stood wide open, and he could see the whirling snow- storm without. It was not very dark. "A pest upon the wind!" said the young man. "It has blown open the door, and the snow has drifted in and covered my feet," and he raised himself upon his elbow. Then he saw that there was a woman in the hut.

She knelt by the side of the old man, his companion, and bent low over him till their faces almost met. White was her face and beautiful; white were her trailing garments; her hair was white with the snow that had fallen upon it. Her hands were stretched forth over the man that slept, and bright icicles hung from her finger- tips. Her breath was quite plainly to be seen as it came from her parted lips. It was like a fair white smoke. Presently she made an end of leaning over the old man, and rose up very tall and slender. Snow fell from her in a shower as she moved.

"That was easy," she murmured, and came to the young man, and sinking down beside him took his hand in hers. If the young man was cold before, he was colder now. He grew numb from head to heel. It seemed to him as if his very blood froze, and his heart was a lump of ice that stood still in his bosom. A deathly sleep stole over him.

"This is my death," he thought. "Can this be all? Thank the gods there is no pain." But the Cold Lady spoke.

"It is only a boy," she said. "A pretty boy," she said, stroking his hair; "I cannot kill him."

"Listen," she said. The young man moaned.

"You must never speak of me, nor of this night," she said. "Not to father, nor mother, nor sister, nor brother, nor to betrothed maid, nor to wedded wife, nor to boy child, nor to girl child, nor to sun, nor moon, nor water, fire, wind, rain, snow. Now swear it."

He swore it. "Fire- wind- rain- snow ..." he murmured, and fell into a deep swoon.

When he came to himself it was high noon, the warm sun shone. A kind countryman held him in his arms and made him drink from a steaming cup.

"Now, boy," said the countryman, "you should do. By the mercy of the gods I came in time, though what brought me to this hut, a good three *ri* out of my way, the August Gods alone know. So you may thank them and your wondrous youth. As for the good old man, your companion, it is a different matter. He is past help. Already his feet have come to the Parting of the Three Ways."

"Alack!" cried the young man. "Alack, for the snow and the storm, and the bitter, bitter night! My friend is dead."

But he said no more then, nor did he when a day's journey brought him home to his own village. For he remembered his oath. And the Cold Lady's words were in his ear.

"You must never speak of me, nor of this night, not to father, nor mother, nor sister, nor brother, nor to betrothed maid, nor to wedded wife, nor to boy child, nor to girl child, nor to sun, nor moon, nor water, fire, wind, rain, snow...."

Some years after this, in the leafy summer time, it chanced that the young man took his walks abroad alone, and as he was returning homewards, about sundown, he was aware of a girl walking in the path a little way before him. It seemed as though she had come some distance, for her robe was kilted up, she wore sandals tied to her feet, and she carried a bundle. Moreover, she drooped and went wearily. It was not strange that the young man should presently come up with her, nor that he should pass the time of day. He saw at once that the girl was very young, fair, and slender.

"Young maiden," he said, "whither are you bound?"

She answered, "Sir, I am bound for Yedo, where I intend to take service. I have a sister there who will find me a place."

"What is your name?" he asked.

"My name is O'Yuki."

"O'Yuki," said the young man, "you look very pale."

"Alas! sir," she murmured, "I faint with the heat of this summer day." And as she stood in the path her slender body swayed, and she slid to his feet in a swoon.

The young man lifted her gently, and carried her in his arms to his mother's house. Her head lay upon his breast, and as he looked upon her face, he shivered slightly.

"All the same," he said to himself, "these summer days turn chilly about sundown, or so it seems to me."

When O'Yuki was recovered of her swoon, she thanked the young man and his mother sweetly for their kindness, and as she had little strength to continue her journey, she passed the night in their house. In truth she passed many nights there, and the streets of Yedo never knew her, for the young man grew to love her, and made her his wife ere many moons were out. Daily she became more beautiful- fair she was, and white. Her little hands, for all she used them for work in the house and work in the fields, were as white as jasmine flowers; the hot sun could not burn her neck, or her pale and delicate cheek. In the fulness of time she bore seven children, all as fair as she, and they grew up tall and strong with straight noble limbs; their equal could not be found upon that country- side. Their mother loved them, reared them, laboured for them. In spite of passing years, in spite of the joys and pains of motherhood, she looked like a slender maiden; there came no line upon her forehead, no dimness to her eyes, and no grey hairs.

All the women of the place marvelled at these things, and talked of them till they were tired. But O'Yuki's husband was the happiest man for miles round, what with his fair wife and his fair children. Morning and evening he prayed and said, "Let not the gods visit it upon me if I have too much joy."

On a certain evening in winter, O'Yuki, having put her children to bed and warmly covered them, was with her husband in the next room. The charcoal glowed in the *hibachi*; all the doors of the house were closely shut, for it was bitter cold, and outside the first big flakes of a snow- storm had begun to fall. O'Yuki stitched diligently at little bright-coloured garments. An *andon* stood on the floor beside her, and its light fell full upon her face.

Her husband looked at her, musing....

"Dear," he said, "when I look at you to-night I am reminded of an adventure that came to me many years since."

O'Yuki spoke not at all, but stitched diligently.

"It was an adventure or a dream," said the man her husband, "and which it was I cannot tell. Strange it was as a dream, yet I think I did not sleep."

O'Yuki went on sewing.

"Then, only then, I saw a woman, who was as beautiful as you are and as white... indeed, she was very like you."

"Tell me about her," said O'Yuki, not lifting her eyes from her work.

"Why," said the man, "I have never spoken of her to anybody." Yet he spoke then to his undoing. He told of his journey, and how he and his companion, being benighted in a snow- storm, took shelter in a hut. He spoke of the white Cold Lady, and of how his friend had died in her chill embrace.

"Then she came to my side and leaned over me, but she said, 'It is only a boy... a pretty boy... I cannot kill him.' Gods! How cold she was... how cold.... Afterwards she made me swear, before she left me she made me swear...."

"You must never speak of me, nor of this night," O'Yuki said, "not to father, nor mother, nor brother, nor sister, nor to betrothed maid, nor to wedded wife, nor to boy child, nor to girl child, nor to sun, nor moon, nor water, fire, wind, rain, snow. All this you swore to me, my husband, even to me. And after all these years you have broken your oath. Unkind, unfaithful, and untrue!" She folded her work together and laid it aside. Then she went to where the children were, and bent her face over each in turn.

The eldest murmured "Cold... Cold ..." so she drew the quilt up over his shoulder.

The youngest cried, "Mother"... and threw out his little arms.

She said, "I have grown too cold to weep any more."

With that she came back to her husband. "Farewell," she said. "Even now I cannot kill you for my little children's sakes. Guard them well."

The man lifted up his eyes and saw her. White was her face and beautiful; white were her trailing garments; her hair was white as it were with snow that had fallen upon it. Her breath was quite plainly to be seen as it came from her parted lips. It was like a fair white smoke.

"Farewell! Farewell!" she cried, and her voice grew thin and chill like a piercing winter wind. Her form grew vague as a snow wreath or a white vaporous cloud. For an instant it hung upon the air. Then it rose slowly through the smoke- hole in the ceiling and was no more seen.

The Fire Quest

The Wise Poet sat reading by the light of his taper. It was a night of the seventh month. The cicala sang in the flower of the pomegranate, the frog sang by the pond. The moon was out and all the stars, the air was heavy and sweet- scented. But the Poet was not happy, for moths came by the score to the light of his taper; not moths only, but cockchafers and dragon- flies with their wings rainbow- tinted. One and all they came upon the Fire Quest; one and all they burned their bright wings in the flame and so died. And the Poet was grieved.

"Little harmless children of the night," he said, "why will you still fly upon the Fire Quest? Never, never can you attain, yet you strive and die. Foolish ones, have you never heard the story of the Firefly Queen?"

The moths and the cockchafers and the dragon- flies fluttered about the taper and paid him no heed.

"They have never heard it," said the Poet; "yet it is old enough. Listen:

"The Firefly Queen was the brightest and most beautiful of small things that fly. She dwelt in the heart of a rosy lotus. The lotus grew on a still lake, and it swayed to and fro upon the lake's bosom while the Firefly Queen slept within. It was like the reflection of a star in the water.

"You must know, oh, little children of the night, that the Firefly Queen had many suitors. Moths and cockchafers and dragon-flies innumerable flew to the lotus on the lake. And their hearts were filled with passionate love. 'Have pity, have pity,' they cried, 'Queen of the Fireflies, Bright Light of the Lake.' But the Firefly Queen sat and smiled and shone. It seemed that she was not sensible of the incense of love that arose about her.

"At last she said, 'Oh, you lovers, one and all, what make you here idly, cumbering my lotus house? Prove your love, if you love me indeed. Go, you lovers, and bring me fire, and then I will answer.'

"Then, oh, little children of the night, there was a swift whirr of wings, for the moths and the cockchafers and the dragon- flies innumerable swiftly departed upon the Fire Quest. But the Firefly Queen laughed. Afterwards I will tell you the reason of her laughter.

"So the lovers flew here and there in the still night, taking with them their desire. They found lighted lattices ajar and entered forthwith. In one chamber there was a girl who took a love- letter from her pillow and read it in tears, by the light of a taper. In another a woman sat holding the light close to a mirror, where she looked and painted her face. A great white moth put out the trembling candle- flame with his wings.

"'Alack! I am afraid,' shrieked the woman; 'the horrible dark!'

"In another place there lay a man dying. He said, 'For pity's sake light me the lamp, for the black night falls.'

"'We have lighted it,' they said, 'long since. It is close beside you, and a legion of moths and dragon- flies flutter about it.'

"'I cannot see anything at all,' murmured the man.

"But those that flew on the Fire Quest burnt their frail wings in the fire. In the morning they lay dead by the hundred and were swept away and forgotten.

"The Firefly Queen was safe in her lotus bower with her beloved, who was as bright as she, for he was a great lord of the Fireflies. No need had he to go upon the Fire Quest. He carried the living flame beneath his wings.

"Thus the Firefly Queen deceived her lovers, and therefore she laughed when she sent them from her on a vain adventure."

"Be not deceived," cried the Wise Poet, "oh, little children of the night. The Firefly Queen is always the same. Give over the Fire Quest."

But the moths and the cockchafers and the dragon- flies paid no heed to the words of the Wise Poet. Still they fluttered about his taper, and they burnt their bright wings in the flame and so died.

Presently the Poet blew out the light. "I must needs sit in the dark," he said; "it is the only way."

A Legend of Kwannon

In the days of the gods, Ama- no- Hashidate was the Floating Bridge of Heaven. By way of this bridge came the deities from heaven to earth, bearing their jewelled spears, their great bows and heavenly- feathered arrows, their wonder robes and their magic mirrors. Afterwards, when the direct way was closed that had been between earth and heaven, and the deities walked no more upon the Land of Fresh Rice Ears, the people still called a place Ama- no- Hashidate, for the sake of happy memory. This place is one of the Three Fair Views of Yamato. It is where a strip of land runs out into the blue sea, like a floating bridge covered with dark pine trees.

There was a holy man of Kioto called Saion Zenji. He had followed the Way of the Gods from his youth up. He was also a disciple of the great Buddha; well versed was he in doctrines and philosophies; he knew the perils of illusion and the ineffable joys of Nirvana. Long hours would he pass in mystic meditation, and many of the Scriptures he had by heart. When he was on a pilgrimage he came to Ama- no- Hashidate, and he offered up thanks because the place was so lovely in his eyes.

He said, "The blind and ignorant have it that trees and rocks and the green sea- water are not sentient things, but the wise know that they also sing aloud and praise the Tathagata. Here will I take up my rest, and join my voice with theirs, and will not see my home again."

So Saion Zenji, the holy man, climbed Nariai- San, the mountain over against Amano- Hashidate. And when he had come to the place of the Lone Pine, he built him a shrine to Kwannon the Merciful, and a hut to cover his own head.

All day he chanted the Holy Sutras. From dawn to eventide he sang, till his very being was exalted and seemed to float in an ecstasy of praise. Then his voice grew so loud and clear that it was a marvel. The blue campanula of the mountain in reverence bowed its head; the great white lily distilled incense from its deep heart; the cicala shrilled aloud; the Forsaken Bird gave a long note from the thicket. About the hermit's hut there fluttered dragon- flies and butterflies innumerable, which are the souls of the happy dead. In the far valleys the peasant people were comforted in their toil, whether they planted out the green young rice, or gathered in the ears. The sun and the wind were tempered, and the rain fell softly upon their faces. Ever and again they climbed the steep hillside to kneel at the shrine of Kwannon the Merciful, and to speak with the holy man, whose wooden bowl they would fill with rice or millet, or barley- meal or beans. Sometimes he came down and went through the villages, where he soothed the sick and touched the little children. Folks said that his very garments shone.

Now in that country there came a winter season the like of which there had not been within the memory of man. First came the wind blowing wildly from the north, and then came the snow in great flakes which never ceased to fall for the period of nine days. All the folk of the valleys kept within doors as warm as might be, and those that had their winter stores fared none so ill. But, ah me, for the bitter cold upon the heights of Nariai-San! At the Lone Pine, and about the hermit's hut, the snow was piled and drifted. The shrine of Kwannon the Merciful could no more be seen. Saion Zenji, the holy man, lived for some time upon the food that was in his wooden bowl. Then he drew about him the warm garment of thought, and passed many days in meditation, which was meat and drink and sleep to him. Howbeit, even his clear spirit could not utterly dispel the clouds of illusion. At length it came to earth and all the man trembled with bodily weakness.

"Forgive me, O Kwannon the Merciful," said Saion Zenji; "but verily it seems to me that if I have no food I die."

Slowly he rose, and painfully he pushed open the door of his hut. The snow had ceased, it was clear and cold. White were the branches of the Lone Pine, and all white the Floating Bridge.

"Forgive me, O Kwannon the Merciful," said Saion Zenji; "I know not the reason, but I am loath to depart and be with the Shades of Yomi. Save me this life, O Kwannon the Merciful."

Turning, he beheld a dappled hind lying on the snow, newly dead of the cold. He bowed his head. "Poor gentle creature," he said, "never more shalt thou run in the hills, and nibble the grass and the sweet flowers." And he stroked the hind's soft flank, sorrowing.

"Poor deer, I would not eat thy flesh. Is it not forbidden by the Law of the Blessed One? Is it not forbidden by the word of Kwannon the Merciful?" Thus he mused. But even as he mused he seemed to hear a voice that spoke to him, and the voice said:

"Alas, Saion Zenji, if thou die of hunger and cold, what shall become of my people, the poor folk of the valleys? Shall they not be comforted any more by the Sutras of the Tathagata? Break the law to keep the law, beloved, thou that countest the world well lost for a divine song."

Then presently Saion Zenji took a knife, and cut him a piece of flesh from the side of the dappled hind. And he gathered fir cones and made a little fire and cooked the deer's flesh in an iron pot. When it was ready he ate half of it. And his strength came to him again, and he opened his lips and sang praises to the Tathagata, and the very embers of the dying fire leapt up in flame to hear him.

"Howbeit I must bury the poor deer," said Saion Zenji. So he went to the door of his hut. But look where he might no deer nor dappled hind did he see, nor yet the mark of one in the deep snow.

"It is passing strange," he said, and wondered.

As soon as might be, up came the poor folk from the valley to see how their hermit had fared through the snow and the stormy weather. "The gods send he be not dead of cold or hunger," they said one to another. But they found him chanting in his hut, and he told them how he had eaten of the flesh of a dappled hind and was satisfied.

"I cut but a hand's breadth of the meat," he said, "and half of it is yet in the iron pot."

But when they came to look in the pot, they found there no flesh of deer, but a piece of cedar wood gilded upon the one side. Marvelling greatly, they carried it to the shrine of Kwannon the Merciful, and when they had cleared away the deep snow, all of them went in to worship. There smiled the image of the sweet heavenly lady, golden among her golden flowers. In her right side there was a gash where the gilded wood was cut away. Then the poor folk from the valley reverently brought that which they had found in the hermit's pot, and set it in the gash. And immediately the wound was healed and the smooth gold shone over the place. All the people fell on their faces, but the hermit stood singing the high praise of Kwannon the Merciful.

The sun set in glory. The valley folk crept softly from the shrine and went down to their own homes. The cold moon and the stars shone upon the Lone Pine and the Floating Bridge and the sea. Through a rent in the shrine's roof they illumined the face of Kwannon the Merciful, and made visible her manifold arms of love. Yet Saion Zenji, her servant, stood before her singing in an ecstasy, with tears upon his face:

"O wonder- woman, strong and beautiful, Tender-hearted, pitiful, and thousand- armed! Thou hast fed me with thine own flesh- Mystery of mysteries! Poor dead dappled hind thou cam'st to me; In the deep of mine own heart thou spoke to me To keep, yet break, and breaking, keep thy law- Mystery of mysteries! Kwannon, the Merciful Lady, stay with me, Save me from the perils of illusion; Let me not be afraid of the snow or the Lone Pine. Mystery of mysteries- Thou hast refused Nirvana, Help me that I may lose the world, content, And sing the Divine Song."

The Espousal of the Rat's Daughter

Mr. Nedzumi, the Rat, was an important personage in the hamlet where he lived- at least he was so in his own and his wife's estimation. This was in part, of course, due to the long line of ancestors from whom he was descended, and to their intimate association with the gods of Good Fortune. For, be it remembered, his ancestry went back into a remote past, in fact as far as time itself; for had not one of his race been selected as the first animal in the cycle of the hours, precedence being even given him over the dragon, the tiger, and the horse? As to his intimacy with the gods, had not one of his forebears been the chosen companion of the great Daikoku, the most revered and the most beneficent of the gods of Good Fortune?

Mr. Rat was well- to- do in life. His home had for generations been established in a snug, warm and cosy bank, hard by one of the most fertile rice- fields on the country- side, where crops never failed, and where in spring he could nibble his fill of the young green shoots, and in autumn gather into his storerooms supplies of the ripened grain sufficient for all his wants during the coming winter.

For his needs were not great.
Entertainment cost him but little, and, unlike his fellows, he had the smallest of families, in fact a family of one only.

But, as regards that one, quality more than compensated for quantity, for it consisted of a daughter, of a beauty unsurpassed in the whole province. He himself had been the object of envy in his married life, for he had had the good fortune to marry into a family of a very select piebald breed, which seldom condescended to mix its blood with the ordinary self- coloured tribe, and now his daughter had been born a peerless white, and had received the name of Yuki, owing to her resemblance to pure snow.

It is little wonder, then, that as she grew up beautiful in form and feature, her father's ambitions were fired, and that he aspired to marry her to the highest in the land.

As it happened, the hamlet where he lived was not very far removed from a celebrated temple, and Mr. Rat, having been brought up in the odour of sanctity, had all his life long been accustomed to make pilgrimages to the great shrine. There he had formed the acquaintance of an old priest, who was good enough to provide for him out of the temple offerings in return for gossip as to the doings of his village, which happened to be that in which the priest had been born and bred. To him the rat had often unburdened his mind, and the old priest had come to see his friend's self- importance and his little weaknesses, and had in vain impressed upon him the virtues of humility.

Now Mr. Rat could find no one amongst his village companions to inform him where to attain what had now become an insatiable desire, namely, a fine marriage for his daughter. So he turned to the temple custodian for advice, and one summer morn found him hammering on the gong which summoned his friend the priest.

"Welcome, Mr. Rat; to what am I indebted for your visit?" said the old priest, for experience had shown him that his friend seldom came so far afield unless he had some request to make.

Thereupon Mr. Rat unburdened himself of all that was in his mind, of his aspiration, and of the difficulty he had in ascertaining in what manner he could obtain it.

Nor did the priest immediately satisfy him, for he said the matter was a difficult one, and would require much consideration. However, on the third day the oracle gave answer as follows: "There is no doubt that apart from the gods there is no one so powerful, or who exercises so beneficent a rule over us, as His Majesty the Sun. Had I a daughter, and did I aspire to such heights for her as you do, I should make my suit to him, and I should take the opportunity of so doing when he comes down to our earth at sundown, for then it is that he decks himself in his most gorgeous apparel; moreover, he is more readily approached when his day's work is done, and he is about to take his well- earned rest. Were I you I would lose no time, but present myself in company with your honourable wife and daughter to him this very evening at the end of the great Cryptomeria Avenue at the hour when he especially honours it by flooding it with his beams."

"A thousand thanks," said Mr. Rat. "No time is to be lost if I am to get my folk together at the time and place you mention."

"Good fortune to you," said the priest; "may I hail you the next time I see you as father- in- law to His Majesty the Sun."

At the appointed hour parents and daughter were to be seen in the avenue, robed in their finest clothes; and as the sun came earthwards and his rays illumined the gloom under the great pines, Mr. Rat, noway abashed, addressed His Majesty and at once informed him of his desire.

His Majesty, evidently considering that one business personage addressing another should not waste time in beating about the bush, replied as follows: "I am extremely beholden to you for your kind intention of allowing me to wed your honourable and beautiful daughter, O Yuki San, but may I ask your reason for selecting me to be your honourable son- in- law?"

To this Mr. Rat replied, "We have determined to marry our daughter to whoever is the most powerful personage in the world, and that is why we desire to offer her to you in marriage."

"Yes," said His Majesty, "you are certainly not without reason in imagining me to be the most august and powerful person in the world; but, unfortunately, it has been my misfortune to discover that there is one other even more powerful than myself, against whose plottings I have no power. It is to him that you should very certainly marry your daughter."

"And may we honourably ask you who that potentate may be?" said Mr. Rat.

"Certainly," rejoined the Sun. "It is the Cloud. Oftentimes when I have set myself to illumine the world he comes across my path and covers my face so that my subjects may not see me, and so long as he does this I am altogether in his power. If, therefore, it is the most powerful personage in the world whom you seek for your daughter, the honourable O Yuki San, you must bestow her on no one else than the Cloud."

It required little consideration for both father and mother to see the wisdom of the Sun's advice, and upon his suggestion they determined to wait on the Cloud at the very earliest opportunity, and at an hour before he rose from his bed, which he usually made on the slopes of a mountain some leagues removed from their village. So they set out, and a long journey they had, so long that Mr. Rat decided that if he was to present his daughter when she was looking her best, the journey must not be hurried. Consequently, instead of arriving at early dawn, it was full afternoon when they neared the summit where the Cloud was apparently wrapped in slumber. But he roused himself as he saw the family approaching, and bade them welcome in so urbane a manner that the Rat at once proceeded to lay his request before him.

To this the Cloud answered, "I am indeed honoured by your condescension in proposing that I should marry your beauteous daughter, O Yuki San. It is quite true, as His August Majesty the Sun says, that when I so desire I have the strength to stay him from exercising his power upon his subjects, and I should much esteem the privilege of wedding your daughter. But as you would single out for that honour the most powerful person in the world, you must seek out His Majesty the Wind, against whom I have no strength, for as soon as he competes with me for supremacy I must fain fly away to the ends of the earth."

"You surprise me," said the Rat, "but I take your word for it. I would, therefore, ask you whether His Majesty the Wind will be this way shortly, and where I may best meet him."

"I am afraid I cannot tell you at the moment when he is likely to be this way. He usually announces his coming by harrying some of my subjects who act as my outposts, but, as you see, they are now all resting quietly. His Majesty is at this moment, I believe, holding a court far out in the Eastern Seas. Were I you I would go down to the seashore and await his coming. He is often somewhat inclined to be short- tempered by the time he gets up into these mountainous parts, owing to the obstructions he has met with on his journey, and he will have had few of these vexatious annoyances during his ride over the sea."

Now, although from the slopes of the mountain the sea looked not very far distant, it was in reality a long way for a delicately-nurtured young lady such as Yuki, and every mile of the journey that she had to traverse increased her querulousness. Her father had often boasted of the journeys that he had taken down to the coast, free of cost, concealed in a truck- load of rice, and she would take no excuses that there was no railway to the point at which they were to await His Highness the Wind, although had there been it would never have done for a party engaged on such an embassy to ride in a railway truck. Nor was her humour improved by the time they had to wait in the very second- rate accommodation afforded by a fishing hamlet, as none of them were accustomed to a fish fare. But after many days there were signs that the great personage was arriving, and they watched with some trepidation his passage over the sea, although when, in due time, he neared the shore they could hardly credit the Cloud's assurance as to his strength, for he seemed the personification of all that was gentle; and Madame Rat at once interposed the remark that you should never judge a person's character by what you hear, and that the Cloud evidently owed the Wind a grudge.

So the Rat at once unburdened himself to the Wind as it came over the water towards him, making its face ripple with smiles. And the Wind itself was in the fairest good humour and addressed the Rat as follows: "Mr. Cloud is a flatterer, and knows full well that I have no power against him when he really comes up against me in one of his thunderous moods. To call me the most powerful person in the world is nonsense. Where do you come from? Why, in that very village there is one stronger than me, namely, the high wall that fences in the house of your good neighbour. If your daughter must fain marry the strongest thing in the world, wed her to the wall. You will find him a very stalwart spouse. I wish you good day. I am sorry I cannot offer you a seat in my chariot, but I am not going in the direction of that wall to- day, else I should have had much pleasure in introducing your honourable self to my powerful antagonist."

By this time the party was getting much disheartened, and the stress of the journey and the chagrin of so many disappointments were beginning to tell on O Yuki San's beauty.

But Mr. Rat said there was nothing for it but to return home; he knew the wall in question very well, but had no idea it stood so high in the world's estimation- he had always thought of it as somewhat of a dullard.

So they trudged homewards, and it was weary work, for the Cloud had hidden the Sun, and the Wind had fretted the Cloud, who showed his ill- humour by discharging a surplusage of moisture he had in his pocket, and they approached their home wet through, bedraggled and worn out. As luck would have it, just as they gained the wall which the wind had singled out for its power, a heavier downpour than ever came on and they were glad to take shelter under the lee of the wall. Now Mr. Wall had always been known for his inquisitive nature, which, it is said, arose from one side of his face never being able to see what was going on on the other; and so hearing his leeward side addressing Mr. Rat, and ascertaining that he had come from the sea, the windward side at once asked whether he had any tidings of that scoundrel the Wind, who was always coming and chafing his complexion.

"Why," said Mr. Rat, "we met him but recently, and he desired to be remembered to you, who, he said, was the strongest person in the world."

"I the strongest! It shows his ignorance. Why, only yesterday your nephew, the big brown rat, because he would not be at the trouble of going round, must needs gnaw a hole through me. The strongest thing in the world! Why, next time the wind comes this way he'll rush through the hole and be telling your nephew that he's the strongest person in the world."

At this moment the rain stopped, the clouds rolled by, and the sun shone out, and Mr. and Mrs. Rat went home congratulating themselves that they had not had to demean themselves by proposing their daughter in marriage to a neighbour with such a false character.

And a month afterwards O Yuki San expressed her determination to marry her cousin, and her parents were fain to give their consent, for had he not proved himself to be the most powerful person in the world?

The Land of Yomi

From the glorious clouds of High Heaven, from the divine ether, the vital essence, and the great concourse of eternal deities, there issued forth the heavenly pair- Izanagi, His Augustness, the Lord of Invitation, and with him, Izanami, Her Augustness, the Lady of Invitation.

Together they stood upon the Floating Bridge of High Heaven, and they looked down to where the mists swirled in confusion beneath their feet. For to them had been given power and commandment to make, consolidate and give birth to the drifting lands. And to this end the august powers had granted them a heavenly jewelled spear. And the two deities, standing upon the Floating Bridge of Heaven, lowered the jewelled spear head- first into chaos, so that the mists were divided. And, as they waited, the brine dripped from the jewels upon the spear- head, and there was formed an island. This is the island of Onogoro.

And His Augustness, the Lord of Invitation, took by the hand Her Augustness, the Lady of Invitation, his lovely Younger Sister, and together they descended to the island that was created. And they made the islands of Japan; the land of Iyo, which is called Lovely Princess; the land of Toyo, which is called Luxuriant Sun Youth; the land of Sanuki, which is called Good Prince Boiled Rice; and Great Yamato, the Luxuriant Island of the Dragon Fly; and many more, of which to tell were weariness.

Furthermore, they gave birth to many myriads of deities to rule over the earth, and the air, and the deep sea; and for every season there were deities, and every place was sacred, for the deities were like the needles of the pine trees in number.

Now, when the time came for the Fire God, Kagu- Tsuchi, to be born, his mother, the Lady Izanami, was burned, and suffered a change; and she laid herself upon the ground. Then Izanagi, the Prince who Invites, asked, "What is it that has come to thee, my lovely Younger Sister?"

And she answered, weeping, "The time of my departure draws near... I go to the land of Yomi."

And His Augustness Izanagi wept aloud, dropping his tears upon her feet and upon her pillow. And all his tears fell down and became deities. Nevertheless, the Lady Izanami departed.

Then His Augustness, the Prince who Invites, was wroth, and lifted his face to High Heaven, and cried, "O Thine Augustness, my lovely Younger Sister, that I should have given thee in exchange for this single child!"

And, drawing the ten- grasp sword that was girded upon him, he slew the Fire God, his child; and binding up his long hair, he followed the Lady Izanami to the entrance of Yomi, the world of the dead. And she, the Princess who Invites, appearing as lovely as she was when alive, came forth to greet him. And she lifted up the curtain of the Palace of Hades that they might speak together.

And the Lord Izanagi said, "I weary for thee, my lovely Younger Sister, and the lands that thou and I created together are not finished making. Therefore come back."

Then the Lady made answer, saying, "My sweet lord, and my spouse, it is very lamentable that thou camest not sooner unto me, for I have eaten of the baked meats of Yomi. Nevertheless, as thou hast dearly honoured me in thy coming here, Thine Augustness, my lovely Elder Brother, if it may be, I will return with thee. I go to lay my desire before the Gods of Yomi. Wait thou here until I come again, and, if thou love me, seek not to look upon me till the time." And so she spoke and left him.

Izanagi sat upon a stone at the entrance of the Palace of Hades until the sun set, and he was weary of that valley of gloom. And because she tarried long, he arose and plucked a comb from the left tress of his hair, and broke off a tooth from one end of the comb, and lighting it to be a torch, he drew back the curtain of the Palace of Yomi. But he saw his beloved lying in corruption, and round about her were the eight deities of Thunder. They are the Fire Thunder, and the Black Thunder, and the Cleaving Thunder, and the Earth Thunder, and the Roaring Thunder, and the Couchant Thunder, and the Young Thunder. And by her terrible head was the Great Thunder.

And Izanagi, being overawed, turned to flee away, but Izanami arose and cried, "Thou hast put me to shame, for thou hast seen my defilement. Now I will see thine also."

And she called to her the Hideous Females of Yomi, and bade them take and slay His Augustness, the Lord who Invites. But he ran for his life, in the gloom stumbling upon the rocks of the valley of Yomi. And tearing the vine wreath from his long hair he flung it behind him, and it fell to the ground and became many bunches of grapes, which the Hideous Females stayed to devour. And he fled on. But the Females of Yomi still pursued him; so then he took a multitudinous and close- toothed comb from the right tresses of his long hair, and cast it behind him. When it touched the ground it became a groove of bamboo shoots, and again the females stayed to devour; and Izanagi fled on, panting.

But, in her wrath and despair, his Younger Sister sent after him the Eight Thunders, together with a thousand and five hundred warriors of Hades; yet he, the Prince of Invitation, drew the ten- grasp sword that was augustly girded upon him, and brandishing it behind him gained at last the base of the Even Pass of Hades, the black mouth of Yomi. And he plucked there three peaches that grew upon a tree, and smote his enemies that they all fled back; and the peaches were called Their Augustnesses, Great Divine Fruit.

Then, last of all, his Younger Sister, the Princess who Invites, herself came out to pursue. So Izanagi took a rock which could not have been lifted by a thousand men, and placed it between them in the Even Pass of Hades. And standing behind the rock, he pronounced a leave- taking and words of separation. But, from the farther side of the rock, Izanami called to him, "My lovely Elder Brother, Thine Augustness, of small avail shall be thy making of lands, and thy creating of deities, for I, with my powers, shall strangle every day a thousand of thy people."

So she cried, taunting him.

But he answered her, "My lovely Younger Sister, Thine Augustness, if thou dost so, I shall cause, in one day, fifteen hundred to be born. Farewell."

So Her Augustness, the Lady who Invites, is called the Queen of the Dead.

But the great lord, His Highness, the Prince who Invites, departed, crying, "Horror! Horror! Horror! I have come to a hideous and polluted land." And he lay still by the riverside, until such time as he should recover strength to perform purification.

The Spring Lover and the Autumn Lover

This is a story of the youth of Yamato, when the gods still walked upon the Land of the Reed Plains and took pleasure in the fresh and waving rice- ears of the country- side.

There was a lady having in her something of earth and something of heaven. She was a king's daughter. She was augustly radiant and renowned. She was called the Dear Delight of the World, the Greatly Desired, the Fairest of the Fair. She was slender and strong, at once mysterious and gay, fickle yet faithful, gentle yet hard to please. The gods loved her, but men worshipped her.

The coming of the Dear Delight was on this wise. Prince Ama Boko had a red jewel of one of his enemies. The jewel was a peace-offering. Prince Ama Boko set it in a casket upon a stand. He said, "This is a jewel of price." Then the jewel was transformed into an exceeding fair lady. Her name was the Lady of the Red Jewel, and Prince Ama Boko took her to wife. There was born to them one only daughter, who was the Greatly Desired, the Fairest of the Fair.

It is true that eighty men of name came to seek her hand. Princes they were, and warriors, and deities. They came from near and they came from far. Across the Sea Path they came in great ships, white sails or creaking oars, with brave and lusty sailors. Through the forests dark and dangerous they made their way to the Princess, the Greatly Desired; or lightly, lightly they descended by way of the Floating Bridge in garments of glamour and silver- shod. They brought their gifts with them- gold, fair jewels upon a string, light garments of feathers, singing birds, sweet things to eat, silk cocoons, oranges in a basket. They brought minstrels and singers and dancers and tellers of tales to entertain the Princess, the Greatly Desired.

As for the Princess, she sat still in her white bower with her maidens about her. Passing rich was her robe, and ever and anon her maidens spread it afresh over the mats, set out her deep sleeves, or combed her long hair with a golden comb.

Round about the bower was a gallery of white wood, and here the suitors came and knelt in the presence of their liege lady.

Many and many a time the carp leapt in the garden fish- pond. Many and many a time a scarlet pomegranate flower fluttered and dropped from the tree. Many and many a time the lady shook her head and a lover went his way, sad and sorry.

Now it happened that the God of Autumn went to try his fortune with the Princess. He was a brave young man indeed. Ardent were his eyes; the colour flamed in his dark cheek. He was girded with a sword that ten men could not lift. The chrysanthemums of autumn burned upon his coat in cunning broidery. He came and bent his proud head to the very ground before the Princess, then raised it and looked her full in the eyes. She opened her sweet red lips- waited- said nothing- but shook her head.

So the God of Autumn went forth from her presence, blinded with his bitter tears.

He found his younger brother, the God of Spring.

"How fares it with you, my brother?" said the God of Spring.

"Ill, ill indeed, for she will not have me. She is the proud lady. Mine is the broken heart."

"Ah, my brother!" said the God of Spring.

"You'd best come home with me, for all is over with us," said the God of Autumn.

But the God of Spring said, "I stay here."

"What," cried his brother, "is it likely, then, that she will take you if she'll have none of me? Will she love the smooth cheeks of a child and flout the man full grown? Will you go to her, brother? She'll laugh at you for your pains."

"Still I will go," said the God of Spring.

"A wager! A wager!" the God of Autumn cried. "I'll give you a cask of *saké* if you win her- *saké* for the merry feast of your wedding. If you lose her, the *saké* will be for me. I'll drown my grief in it."

"Well, brother," said the God of Spring, "I take the wager. You'll have your *saké* like enough indeed."

"And so I think," said the God of Autumn, and went his ways.

Then the young God of Spring went to his mother, who loved him.

"Do you love me, my mother?" he said.

She answered, "More than a hundred existences."

"Mother," he said, "get me for my wife the Princess, the Fairest of the Fair. She is called the Greatly Desired; greatly, oh, greatly, do I desire her."

"You love her, my son?" said his mother.

"More than a hundred existences," he said.

"Then lie down, my son, my best beloved, lie down and sleep, and I will work for you."

So she spread a couch for him, and when he was asleep she looked on him.

"Your face," she said, "is the sweetest thing in the world."

There was no sleep for her the live-long night, but she went swiftly to a place she knew of, where the wistaria drooped over a still pool. She plucked her sprays and tendrils and brought home as much as she could carry. The wistaria was white and purple, and you must know it was not yet in flower, but hidden in the unopened bud. From it she wove magically a robe. She fashioned sandals also, and a bow and arrows.

In the morning she waked the God of Spring.

"Come, my son," she said, "let me put this robe on you."

The God of Spring rubbed his eyes. "A sober suit for courting," he said. But he did as his mother bade him. And he bound the sandals on his feet, and slung the bow and the arrows in their quiver on his back.

"Will all be well, my mother?" he said.

"All will be well, beloved," she answered him.

So the God of Spring came before the Fairest of the Fair. And one of her maidens laughed and said:

"See, mistress, there comes to woo you to-day only a little plain boy, all in sober grey."

But the Fairest of the Fair lifted up her eyes and looked upon the God of Spring. And in the same moment the wistaria with which he was clothed burst into flower. He was sweet- scented, white and purple from head to heel.

The Princess rose from the white mats.

"Lord," she said, "I am yours if you will have me."

Hand in hand they went together to the mother of the God of Spring.

"Ah, my mother," he said, "what shall I do now? My brother the God of Autumn is angry with me. He will not give me the *saké* I have won from him in a wager. Great is his rage. He will seek to take our lives."

"Be still, beloved," said his mother, "and fear not."

She took a cane of hollow bamboo, and in the hollow she put salt and stones; and when she had wrapped the cane round with leaves, she hung it in the smoke of the fire. She said:

"The green leaves fade and die. So you must do, my eldest born, the God of Autumn. The stone sinks in the sea, so must you sink. You must sink, you must fail, like the ebb tide."

Now the tale is told, and all the world knows why Spring is fresh and merry and young, and Autumn the saddest thing that is.

The Strange Story of the Golden Comb

In ancient days two *samurai* dwelt in Sendai of the North. They were friends and brothers in arms.

Hasunuma one was named, and the other Saito. Now it happened that a daughter was born to the house of Hasunuma, and upon the selfsame day, and in the selfsame hour, there was born to the house of Saito a son. The boy child they called Konojo, and the girl they called Aiko, which means the Child of Love.

Or ever a year had passed over their innocent heads the children were betrothed to one another. And as a token the wife of Saito gave a golden comb to the wife of Hasunuma, saying: "For the child's hair when she shall be old enough." Aiko's mother wrapped the comb in a handkerchief, and laid it away in her chest. It was of gold lacquer, very fine work, adorned with golden dragon- flies.

This was very well; but before long misfortune came upon Saito and his house, for, by sad mischance, he aroused the ire of his feudal lord, and he was fain to fly from Sendai by night, and his wife was with him, and the child. No man knew where they went, or had any news of them, nor of how they fared, and for long, long years Hasunuma heard not one word of them.

The child Aiko grew to be the loveliest lady in Sendai. She had longer hair than any maiden in the city, and she was the most graceful dancer ever seen. She moved as a wave of the sea, or a cloud of the sky, or the wild bamboo grass in the wind. She had a sister eleven moons younger than she, who was called Aiyamé, or the Water Iris; and she was the second loveliest lady in Sendai. Aiko was white, but Aiyamé was brown, quick, and light, and laughing. When they went abroad in the streets of Sendai, folk said, "There go the moon and the south wind."

Upon an idle summer day when all the air was languid, and the cicala sang ceaselessly as he swung on the pomegranate bough, the maidens rested on the cool white mats of their lady mother's bower. Their dark locks were loose, and their slender feet were bare. They had between them an ancient chest of red lacquer, a Bride Box of their lady mother's, and in the chest they searched and rummaged for treasure.

"See, sister," said Aiyamé, "here are scarlet thongs, the very thing for my sandals... and what is this? A crystal rosary, I declare! How beautiful!"

Aiko said, "My mother, I pray you give me this length of violet silk, it will make me very fine undersleeves to my new grey gown; and, mother, let me have the crimson for a petticoat; and surely, mother, you do not need this little bit of brocade?"

"And what an *obi*," cried Aiyamé, as she dragged it from the chest, "grass green and silver!" Springing lightly up, she wound the length about her slender body. "Now behold me for the finest lady in all Sendai. Very envious shall be the daughter of the rich Hachiman, when she sees this wonder *obi*; but I shall be calm and careless, and say, looking down thus humbly, 'Your pardon, noble lady, that I wear this foolish trifling *obi*, unmeet for your great presence!' Mother, mother, give me the *obi*."

"Arah! Arah! Little pirates!" said the mother, and smiled.

Aiko thrust her hand to the bottom of the chest. "Here is something hard," she murmured, "a little casket wrapped in a silken handkerchief. How it smells of orris and ancient spices!- now what may it be?" So saying, she unwound the kerchief and opened the casket. "A golden comb!" she said, and laid it on her knee.

"Give it here, child," cried the mother quickly; "it is not for your eyes."

But the maiden sat quite still, her eyes upon the golden comb. It was of gold lacquer, very fine work, adorned with golden dragon-flies.

For a time the maiden said not a word, nor did her mother, though she was troubled; and even the light Lady of the South Wind seemed stricken into silence, and drew the scarlet sandal thongs through and through her fingers.

"Mother, what of this golden comb?" said Aiko at last.

"My sweet, it is the love- token between you and Konojo, the son of Saito, for you two were betrothed in your cradles. But now it is full fifteen years since Saito went from Sendai in the night, he and all his house, and left no trace behind."

"Is my love dead?" said Aiko.

"Nay, that I know not- but he will never come; so, I beseech you, think no more of him, my pretty bird. There, get you your fan, and dance for me and for your sister."

Aiko first set the golden comb in her hair. Then she flung open her fan to dance. She moved like a wave of the sea, or a cloud of the sky, or the wild bamboo grass in the wind.

She had not danced long before she dropped the fan, with a long cry, and she herself fell her length upon the ground. From that hour she was in a piteous way, and lay in her bed sighing, like a maid lovelorn and forsaken. She could not eat nor sleep; she had no pleasure in life. The sunrise and the sound of rain at night were nothing to her any more. Not her father, nor her mother, nor her sister, the Lady of the South Wind, were able to give her any ease.

Presently she turned her face to the wall. "It is more than I can understand," she said, and so died.

When they had prepared the poor young maid for her grave, her mother came, crying, to look at her for the last time. And she set the golden comb in the maid's hair, saying:

"My own dear little child, I pray that in other lives you may know happiness. Therefore take your golden token with you; you will have need of it when you meet the wraith of your lover." For she believed that Konojo was dead.

But, alas, for Karma that is so pitiless, one short moon had the maid been in her grave when the brave young man, her betrothed, came to claim her at her father's house.

"Alas and alack, Konojo, the son of Saito, alas, my brave young man, too late you have come! Your joy is turned to mourning, for your bride lies under the green grass, and her sister goes weeping in the moonlight to pour the water of the dead." Thus spoke Hasunuma the *samurai*.

"Lord," said the brave young man, "there are three ways left, the sword, the strong girdle, and the river. These are the short roads to Yomi. Farewell."

But Hasunuma held the young man by the arm. "Nay, then, thou son of Saito," he said, "but hear the fourth way, which is far better. The road to Yomi is short, but it is very dark; moreover, from the confines of that country few return. Therefore stay with me, Konojo, and comfort me in my old age, for I have no sons."

So Konojo entered the household of Hasunuma the *samurai*, and dwelt in the garden house by the gate.

Now in the third month Hasunuma and his wife and the daughter that was left them arose early and dressed them in garments of ceremony, and presently were borne away in *kago*, for to the temple they were bound, and to their ancestral tombs, where they offered prayers and incense the live- long day.

It was bright starlight when they returned, and cold the night was, still and frosty.

Konojo stood and waited at the garden gate. He waited for their home- coming, as was meet. He drew his cloak about him and gave ear to the noises of the evening. He heard the sound of the blind man's whistle, and the blind man's staff upon the stones. Far off he heard a child laugh twice; then he heard men singing in chorus, as men who sing to cheer themselves in their labour, and in the pauses of song he heard the creak, creak of swinging *kago* that the men bore upon their shoulders, and he said, "They come."

"I go to the house of the Beloved, Her plum tree stands by the eaves; It is full of blossom. The dew lies in the heart of the flowers, So they are the drinking-cups of the sparrows. How do you go to your love's house? Even upon the wings of the night wind. Which road leads to your love's house? All the roads in the world."

This was the song of the *kago* men. First the *kago* of Hasunuma the *samurai* turned in at the garden gate, then followed his lady; last came Aiyamé of the South Wind. Upon the roof of her *kago* there lay a blossoming bough.

"Rest well, lady," said Konojo, as she passed, and had no answer back. Howbeit it seemed that some light thing dropped from the *kago*, and fell with a little noise to the ground. He stooped and picked up a woman's comb. It was of gold lacquer, very fine work, adorned with golden dragon- flies. Smooth and warm it lay in the hand of Konojo. And he went his way to the garden house. At the hour of the rat the young *samurai* threw down his book of verse, laid himself upon his bed, and blew out his light. And the selfsame moment he heard a wandering step without.

"And who may it be that visits the garden house by night?" said Konojo, and he wondered. About and about went the wandering feet till at length they stayed, and the door was touched with an uncertain hand.

"Konojo! Konojo!"

"What is it?" said the *samurai*.

"Open, open; I am afraid."

"Who are you, and why are you afraid?"

"I am afraid of the night. I am the daughter of Hasunuma the *samurai*.... Open to me for the love of the gods."

Konojo undid the latch and slid back the door of the garden house to find a slender and drooping lady upon the threshold. He could not see her face, for she held her long sleeve so as to hide it from him; but she swayed and trembled, and her frail shoulders shook with sobbing.

"Let me in," she moaned, and forthwith entered the garden house.

Half smiling and much perplexed, Konojo asked her:

"Are you Aiyamé, whom they call the Lady of the South Wind?"

"I am she."

"Lady, you do me much honour."

"The comb!" she said, "the golden comb!"

As she said this, she threw the veil from her face, and taking the robe of Konojo in both her little hands, she looked into his eyes as though she would draw forth his very soul. The lady was brown and quick and light. Her eyes and her lips were made for laughing, and passing strange she looked in the guise that she wore then.

"The comb!" she said, "the golden comb!"

"I have it here," said Konojo; "only let go my robe, and I will fetch it you."

At this the lady cast herself down upon the white mats in a passion of bitter tears, and Konojo, poor unfortunate, pressed his hands together, quite beside himself.

"What to do?" he said; "what to do?"

At last he raised the lady in his arms, and stroked her little hand to comfort her.

"Lord," she said, as simply as a child, "lord, do you love me?"

And he answered her in a moment, "I love you more than many lives, O Lady of the South Wind."

"Lord," she said, "will you come with me then?"

He answered her, "Even to the land of Yomi," and took her hand.

Forth they went into the night, and they took the road together. By river- side they went, and over plains of flowers; they went by rocky ways, or through the whispering pines, and when they had wandered far enough, of the green bamboos they built them a little house to dwell in. And they were there for a year of happy days and nights.

Now upon a morning of the third month Konojo beheld men with *kago* come swinging through the bamboo grove. And he said:

"What have they to do with us, these men and their *kago*?"

"Lord," said Aiyamé, "they come to bear us to my father's house."

He cried, "What is this foolishness? We will not go."

"Indeed, and we must go," said the lady.

"Go you, then," said Konojo; "as for me, I stay here where I am happy."

"Ah, lord," she said, "ah, my dear, do you then love me less, who vowed to go with me, even to the Land of Yomi?"

Then he did all that she would. And he broke a blossoming bough from a tree that grew near by and laid it upon the roof of her *kago*.

Swiftly, swiftly they were borne, and the *kago* men sang as they went, a song to make labour light.

"I go to the house of the Beloved, Her plum tree stands by the eaves; It is full of blossom. The dew lies in the heart of the flowers, So they are the drinking-cups of the sparrows. How do you go to your love's house? Even upon the wings of the night wind. Which road leads to your love's house? All the roads in the world."

This was the song of the *kago* men.

About nightfall they came to the house of Hasunuma the *samurai*.

"Go you in, my dear lord," said the Lady of the South Wind. "I will wait without; if my father is very wroth with you, only show him the golden comb." And with that she took it from her hair and gave it him. Smooth and warm it lay in his hand. Then Konojo went into the house.

"Welcome, welcome home, Konojo, son of Saito!" cried Hasunuma. "How has it fared with your knightly adventure?"

"Knightly adventure!" said Konojo, and blushed.

"It is a year since your sudden departure, and we supposed that you had gone upon a quest, or in the expiation of some vow laid upon your soul."

"Alas, my good lord," said Konojo, "I have sinned against you and against your house." And he told Hasunuma what he had done.

When he had made an end of his tale:

"Boy," said the *samurai*, "you jest, but your merry jest is ill- timed. Know that my child lies even as one dead. For a year she has neither risen nor spoken nor smiled. She is visited by a heavy sickness and none can heal her."

"Sir," said Konojo, "your child, the Lady of the South Wind, waits in a *kago* without your garden wall. I will fetch her in presently."

Forth they went together, the young man and the *samurai*, but they found no *kago* without the garden wall, no *kago*-bearers and no lady. Only a broken bough of withered blossom lay upon the ground.

"Indeed, indeed, she was here but now!" cried Konojo. "She gave me her comb- her golden comb. See, my lord, here it is."

"What comb is this, Konojo? Where got you this comb that was set in a dead maid's hair, and buried with her beneath the green grass? Where got you the comb of Aiko, the Lady of the Moon, that died for love? Speak, Konojo, son of Saito. This is a strange thing."

Now whilst Konojo stood amazed, and leaned silent and bewildered against the garden wall, a lady came lightly through the trees. She moved as a wave of the sea, or a cloud of the sky, or the wild bamboo grass in the wind.

"Aiyamé," cried the *samurai*, "how are you able to leave your bed?"

The young man said nothing, but fell on his knees beside the garden wall. There the lady came to him and bent so that her hair and her garments overshadowed him, and her eyes held his.

"Lord," she said, "I am the spirit of Aiko your love. I went with a broken heart to dwell with the shades of Yomi. The very dead took pity on my tears. I was permitted to return, and for one short year to inhabit the sweet body of my sister. And now my time is come. I go my ways to the grey country. I shall be the happiest soul in Yomi- I have known you, beloved. Now take me in your arms, for I grow very faint."

With that she sank to the ground, and Konojo put his arms about her and laid her head against his heart. His tears fell upon her forehead.

"Promise me," she said, "that you will take to wife Aiyamé, my sister, the Lady of the South Wind."

"Ah," he cried, "my lady and my love!"

"Promise, promise," she said.

Then he promised.

After a little she stirred in his arms.

"What is it?" he said.

So soft her voice that it did not break the silence but floated upon it.

"The comb," she murmured, "the golden comb."

And Konojo set it in her hair.

A burden, pale but breathing, Konojo carried into the house of Hasunuma and laid upon the white mats and silken cushions. And after three hours a young maid sat up and rubbed her sleepy eyes. She was brown and quick and light and laughing. Her hair was tumbled about her rosy cheeks, unconfined by any braid or comb. She stared first at her father, and then at the young man that was in her bower. She smiled, then flushed, and put her little hands before her face.

"Greeting, O Lady of the South Wind," said Konojo.

The Jelly- Fish takes a Journey

Once upon a time the jelly- fish was a very handsome fellow. His form was beautiful, and round as the full moon. He had glittering scales and fins and a tail as other fishes have, but he had more than these. He had little feet as well, so that he could walk upon the land as well as swim in the sea. He was merry and he was gay, he was beloved and trusted of the Dragon King. In spite of all this, his grandmother always said he would come to a bad end, because he would not mind his books at school. She was right. It all came about in this wise.

The Dragon King was but lately wed when the young Lady Dragon his wife fell very sick. She took to her bed and stayed there, and wise folk in Dragonland shook their heads and said her last day was at hand. Doctors came from far and near, and they dosed her and they bled her, but no good at all could they do her, the poor young thing, nor recover her of her sickness.

The Dragon King was beside himself.

"Heart's Desire," he said to his pale bride, "I would give my life for you."

240

"Little good would it do me," she answered. "Howbeit, if you will fetch me a monkey's liver I will eat it and live."

"A monkey's liver!" cried the Dragon King. "A monkey's liver! You talk wildly, O light of mine eyes. How shall I find a monkey's liver? Know you not, sweet one, that monkeys dwell in the trees of the forest, whilst we are in the deep sea?"

Tears ran down the Dragon Queen's lovely countenance.

"If I do not have the monkey's liver, I shall die," she said.

Then the Dragon went forth and called to him the jelly- fish.

"The Queen must have a monkey's liver," he said, "to cure her of her sickness."

"What will she do with the monkey's liver?" asked the jelly- fish.

"Why, she will eat it," said the Dragon King.

"Oh!" said the jelly- fish.

"Now," said the King, "you must go and fetch me a live monkey. I have heard that they dwell in the tall trees of the forest. Therefore swim quickly, O jelly- fish, and bring a monkey with you back again."

"How will I get the monkey to come back with me?" said the jelly- fish.

"Tell him of all the beauties and pleasures of Dragonland. Tell him he will be happy here and that he may play with mermaids all the day long."

"Well," said the jelly- fish, "I'll tell him that."

Off set the jelly- fish; and he swam and he swam, till at last he reached the shore where grew the tall trees of the forest. And, sure enough, there was a monkey sitting in the branches of a persimmon tree, eating persimmons.

"The very thing," said the jelly- fish to himself; "I'm in luck."

"Noble monkey," he said, "will you come to Dragonland with me?"

"How should I get there?" said the monkey.

"Only sit on my back," said the jelly- fish, "and I'll take you there; you'll have no trouble at all."

"Why should I go there, after all?" said the monkey. "I am very well off as I am."

"Ah," said the jelly- fish, "it's plain that you know little of all the beauties and pleasures of Dragonland. There you will be happy as the day is long. You will win great riches and honour. Besides, you may play with the mermaids from morn till eve."

"I'll come," said the monkey.

And he slipped down from the persimmon tree and jumped on the jelly-fish's back.

When the two of them were about half-way over to Dragonland, the jelly-fish laughed.

"Now, jelly-fish, why do you laugh?"

"I laugh for joy," said the jelly-fish. "When you come to Dragonland, my master, the Dragon King, will get your liver, and give it to my mistress the Dragon Queen to eat, and then she will recover from her sickness."

"My liver?" said the monkey.

"Why, of course," said the jelly-fish.

"Alas and alack," cried the monkey, "I'm grieved indeed, but if it's my liver you're wanting I haven't it with me. To tell you the truth, it weighs pretty heavy, so I just took it out and hung it upon a branch of that persimmon tree where you found me. Quick, quick, let's go back for it."

Back they went, and the monkey was up in the persimmon tree in a twinkling.

"Mercy me, I don't see it at all," he said. "Where can I have mislaid it? I should not be surprised if some rascal has stolen it," he said.

Now if the jelly-fish had minded his books at school, would he have been hoodwinked by the monkey? You may believe not. But his grandmother always said he would come to a bad end.

"I shall be some time finding it," said the monkey. "You'd best be getting home to Dragonland. The King would be loath for you to be out after dark. You can call for me another day. *Sayonara.*"

The monkey and the jelly- fish parted on the best of terms.

The minute the Dragon King set eyes on the jelly- fish, "Where's the monkey?" he said.

"I'm to call for him another day," said the jelly- fish. And he told all the tale.

The Dragon King flew into a towering rage. He called his executioners and bid them beat the jelly- fish.

"Break every bone in his body," he cried; "beat him to a jelly."

Alas for the sad fate of the jelly- fish! Jelly he remains to this very day.

As for the young Dragon Queen, she was fain to laugh when she heard the story.

"If I can't have a monkey's liver I must needs do without it," she said. "Give me my best brocade gown and I will get up, for I feel a good deal better."

Urashima

Urashima was a fisherman of the Inland Sea.

Every night he plied his trade. He caught fishes both great and small, being upon the sea through the long hours of darkness. Thus he made his living.

Upon a certain night the moon shone brightly, making plain the paths of the sea. And Urashima kneeled in his boat and dabbled his right hand in the green water. Low he leaned, till his hair lay spread upon the waves, and he paid no heed to his boat that listed or to his trailing fishing- net. He drifted in his boat till he came to a haunted place. And he was neither waking nor sleeping, for the moon made him mad.

Then the Daughter of the Deep Sea arose, and she took the fisherman in her arms, and sank with him, down, down, to her cold sea cave. She laid him upon a sandy bed, and long did she look upon him. She cast her sea spell upon him, and sang her sea songs to him and held his eyes with hers.

He said, "Who are you, lady?"

She told him, "The Daughter of the Deep Sea."

"Let me go home," he said; "my little children wait and are tired."

"Nay, rather stay with me," she said:

"Urashima, Thou Fisherman of the Inland Sea, Thou art beautiful; Thy long hair is twisted round my heart; Go not from me, Only forget thy home."

"Ah, now," said the fisherman, "let be, for the dear gods' sake.... I would go to mine own."

But she said again:

"Urashima, Thou Fisherman of the Inland Sea, I'll set thy couch with pearl; I'll spread thy couch with seaweed and sea flowers; Thou shalt be King of the Deep Sea, And we will reign together."

"Let me go home," said Urashima; "my little children wait and are tired."

But she said:

"Urashima: Thou Fisherman of the Inland Sea, Never be afraid of the Deep Sea tempest; We will roll rocks about our cavern doors; Neither be afraid of the drowned dead; Thou shalt not die."

"Ah, now," said the fisherman, "let be, for the dear gods' sake.... I would go to mine own."

"Stay with me this one night."

"Nay, not one."

Then the Daughter of the Deep Sea wept, and Urashima saw her tears.

"I will stay with you this one night," he said.

So after the night was passed, she brought him up to the sand and the seashore.

"Are we near your home?" she said.

He told her, "Within a stone's throw."

"Take this," she said, "in memory of me." She gave him a casket of mother- of- pearl; it was rainbow- tinted and its clasps were of coral and of jade.

"Do not open it," she said; "O fisherman, do not open it." And with that she sank and was no more seen, the Daughter of the Deep Sea.

As for Urashima, he ran beneath the pine trees to come to his dear home. And as he went he laughed for joy. And he tossed up the casket to catch the sun.

"Ah, me," he said, "the sweet scent of the pines!" So he went calling to his children with a call that he had taught them, like a sea- bird's note. Soon he said, "Are they yet asleep? It is strange they do not answer me."

Now when he came to his house he found four lonely walls, moss- grown. Nightshade flourished on the threshold, death lilies by the hearth, dianthus and lady fern. No living soul was there.

"Now what is this?" cried Urashima. "Have I lost my wits? Have I left my eyes in the deep sea?"

He sat down upon the grassy floor and thought long. "The dear gods help me!" he said. "Where is my wife, and where are my little children?"

He went to the village, where he knew the stones in the way, and every tiled and tilted eave was to him most familiar; and here he found folk walking to and fro, going upon their business. But they were all strange to him.

"Good morrow," they said, "good morrow, wayfarer. Do you tarry in our town?"

He saw children at their play, and often he put his hand beneath their chins to turn their faces up. Alas! he did it all in vain.

"Where are my little children," he said, "O Lady Kwannon the Merciful? Peradventure the gods know the meaning of all this; it is too much for me."

When sunset came, his heart was heavy as stone, and he went and stood at the parting of the ways outside the town. As men passed by he pulled them by the sleeve:

"Friend," he said, "I ask your pardon, did you know a fisherman of this place called Urashima?"

And the men that passed by answered him, "We never heard of such an one."

There passed by the peasant people from the mountains. Some went a- foot, some rode on patient pack- horses. They went singing their country songs, and they carried baskets of wild strawberries or sheaves of lilies bound upon their backs. And the lilies nodded as they went. Pilgrims passed by, all clad in white, with staves and rice- straw hats, sandals fast bound and gourds of water. Swiftly they went, softly they went, thinking of holy things. And lords and ladies passed by, in brave attire and great array, borne in their gilded *kago*. The night fell.

"I lose sweet hope," said Urashima.

But there passed by an old, old man.

"Oh, old, old man," cried the fisherman, "you have seen many days; know you ought of Urashima? In this place was he born and bred."

Then the old man said, "There was one of that name, but, sir, that one was drowned long years ago. My grandfather could scarce remember him in the time that I was a little boy. Good stranger, it was many, many years ago."

Urashima said, "He is dead?"

"No man more dead than he. His sons are dead and their sons are dead. Good even to you, stranger."

Then Urashima was afraid. But he said, "I must go to the green valley where the dead sleep." And to the valley he took his way.

He said, "How chill the night wind blows through the grass! The trees shiver and the leaves turn their pale backs to me."

He said, "Hail, sad moon, that showest me all the quiet graves. Thou art nothing different from the moon of old."

He said, "Here are my sons' graves and their sons' graves. Poor Urashima, there is no man more dead than he. Yet am I lonely among the ghosts...."

"Who will comfort me?" said Urashima.

The night wind sighed and nothing more.

Then he went back to the seashore. "Who will comfort me?" cried Urashima. But the sky was unmoved, and the mountain waves of the sea rolled on.

Urashima said, "There is the casket." And he took it from his sleeve and opened it. There rose from it a faint white smoke that floated away and out to the far horizon.

"I grow very weary," said Urashima. In a moment his hair turned as white as snow. He trembled, his body shrank, his eyes grew dim.

He that had been so young and lusty swayed and tottered where he stood.

"I am old," said Urashima.

He made to shut the casket lid, but dropped it, saying, "Nay, the vapour of smoke is gone for ever. What matters it?"

He laid down his length upon the sand and died.

Tamamo, the Fox Maiden

A pedlar journeyed with his pack upon the great high- road which leads to the city of Kioto. He found a child sitting all alone by the wayside.

"Well, my little girl," he said, "and what make you all alone by the wayside?"

"What do you," said the child, "with a staff and a pack, and sandals outworn?"

"I am bound for Kioto, and the Mikado's Palace, to sell my gauds to the ladies of the Court."

"Ah," said the child, "take me too."

"What is your name, my little girl?"

"I have no name."

"Whence come you?"

"I come from nowhere."

"You seem to be about seven years old."

"I have no age."

"Why are you here?"

"I have been waiting for you."

"How long have you waited?"

"For more than a hundred years."

The Pedlar laughed.

"Take me to Kioto," said the child.

"You may come if you will," said the Pedlar. So they went their ways together, and in time they came to Kioto and to the

Mikado's Palace. Here the child danced in the august presence of the Son of Heaven. She was as light as the sea- bird upon a wave's crest. When she had made an end of dancing, the Mikado called her to him.

"Little maid," he said, "what guerdon shall I give you? Ask!"

"O Divinely Descended," said the child, "Son of the Gods... I cannot ask.... I am afraid."

"Ask without fear," said the Mikado.

The child murmured, "Let me stay in the bright presence of your Augustness."

"So be it," said the Mikado, and he received the child into his household. And he called her Tamamo.

Very speedily she became mistress of every lovely art. She could sing, and she could play upon any instrument of music. She had more skill in painting than any painter in the land; she was a wonder with the needle and a wonder at the loom. The poetry that she made moved men to tears and to laughter. The many thousand characters were child's play to her, and all the hard philosophies she had at her fingers' ends. She knew Confucius well enough, the Scriptures of Buddha, and the lore of Cathay. She was called the Exquisite

Perfection, the Gold Unalloyed, the Jewel without Flaw.

And the Mikado loved her.

Soon he clean forgot honour and duty and kingly state. Day and night he kept Tamamo by his side. He grew rough and fierce and passionate, so that his servants feared to approach him. He grew sick, listless, and languid, he pined, and his physicians could do nothing for him.

"Alas and alack," they cried, "what ails the Divinely Descended? Of a surety he is bewitched. Woe! woe! for he will die upon our hands."

"Out upon them, every one," cried the Mikado, "for a pack of tedious fools. As for me, I will do my own will and pleasure."

He was mad for love of Tamamo.

He took her to his Summer Palace, where he prepared a great feast in her honour. To the feast were bidden all the highest of the land, princes and lords and ladies of high estate; and, willy- nilly, to the Summer Palace they all repaired, where was the Mikado, wan and wild, and mad with love, and Tamamo by his side, attired in scarlet and cloth of gold. Radiantly fair she was, and she poured the Mikado's *saké* out of a golden flagon.

He looked into her eyes.

"Other women are feeble toys beside you," he said. "There's not a woman here that's fit to touch the end of your sleeve. O Tamamo, how I love you...."

He spoke loudly so that all could hear him, and laughed bitterly when he had spoken.

"My lord... my lord ..." said Tamamo.

Now as the high company sat and feasted, the sky became overcast with black clouds, and the moon and the stars were hid. Suddenly a fearful wind tore through the Summer Palace and put out every torch in the great Hall of Feasting. And the rain came down in torrents. In the pitchy darkness fear and horror fell upon the assembly. The courtiers ran to and fro in a panic, the air was full of cries, the tables were overturned. The dishes and drinking- vessels crashed together, the *saké* spilled and soaked into the white mats. Then a radiance was made visible. It came from the place where Tamamo was, and it streamed in long flames of fire from her body.

The Mikado cried aloud in a terrible voice, "Tamamo! Tamamo! Tamamo!" three times. And when he had done this he fell in a deathly swoon upon the ground.

And for many days he was thus, and he seemed either asleep or dead, and no one could recover him from his swoon.

Then the Wise and Holy Men of the land met together, and when they had prayed to the gods, they called to them Abé Yasu, the Diviner. They said:

"O Abé Yasu, learned in dark things, find out for us the cause, and if it may be, the cure, of our Lord's strange sickness. Perform divination for us, O Abé Yasu."

Then Abé Yasu performed divination, and he came before the Wise Men and said:

"The wine is sweet, but the aftertaste is bitter. Set not your teeth in the golden persimmon, It is rotten at the core. Fair is the scarlet flower of the Death Lily, Pluck it not. What is beauty? What is wisdom? What is love? Be not deceived. They are threads in the fabric of illusion!"

Then the Wise Men said, "Speak out, Abé Yasu, for your saying is dark, and we cannot understand it."

"I will do more than speak," said Abé Yasu. And he spent three days in fasting and in prayer. Then he took the sacred *Gohei* from its place in the Temple, and calling the Wise Men to him he waved the sacred *Gohei* and with it touched each one of them. And together they went to Tamamo's bower, and

256

Abé Yasu took the sacred *Gohei* in his right hand.

Tamamo was in her bower adorning herself, and her maidens were with her.

"My lords," she said, "you come all unbidden. What would you have with me?"

"My lady Tamamo," said Abé Yasu the Diviner, "I have made a song after the fashion of the Chinese. You who are learned in poetry, I pray you hear and judge my song."

"I am in no mood for songs," she said, "with my dear lord lying sick to death."

"Nevertheless, my lady Tamamo, this song of mine you needs must hear."

"Why, then, if I must ..." she said.

Then spoke Abé Yasu:

"The wine is sweet, the aftertaste is bitter. Set not your teeth in the golden persimmon, It is rotten at the core. Fair is the scarlet flower of the Death Lily, Pluck it not. What is beauty? What is wisdom? What is love? Be not deceived. They are threads in the fabric of illusion!"

When Abé Yasu the Diviner had spoken, he came to Tamamo and he touched her with the sacred *Gohei*.

She gave a loud and terrible cry, and on the instant her form was changed into that of a great fox having nine long tails and hair like golden wire. The fox fled from Tamamo's bower, away and away, until it reached the far plain of Nasu, and it hid itself beneath a great black stone that was upon that plain.

But the Mikado was immediately recovered from his sickness.

Soon, strange and terrible things were told concerning the great stone of Nasu. A stream of poisonous water flowed from under it and withered the bright flowers of the plain. All who drank of the stream died, both man and beast. Moreover, nothing could go near the stone and live. The traveller who rested in its shadow arose no more, and the birds that perched upon it fell dead in a moment. People named it the Death Stone, and thus it was called for more than a hundred years.

Then it chanced that Genyo, the High Priest, who was a holy man indeed, took his staff and his begging bowl and went upon a pilgrimage.

When he came to Nasu, the dwellers upon the plain put rice into his bowl.

"O thou Holy Man," they said, "beware the Death Stone of Nasu. Rest not in its shade."

But Genyo, the High Priest, having remained a while in thought, made answer thus:

"Know, my children, what is written in the Book of the Good Law: 'Herbs, trees and rocks shall all enter into Nirvana.'"

With that he took his way to the Death Stone. He burnt incense, he struck the stone with his staff, and he cried, "Come forth, Spirit of the Death Stone; come forth, I conjure thee."

Then there was a great flame of fire and a rending noise, and the Stone burst and split in sunder. From the stone and from the fire there came a woman.

She stood before the Holy Man. She said:

"*I am Tamamo, once called the Proud Perfection; I am the golden- haired Fox; I know the Sorceries of the East; I was worshipped by the Princes of Ind; I was great Cathay's undoing; I was wise and beautiful, Evil incarnate. The power of the Buddha has changed me; I have dwelt in grief for a hundred years; Tears have washed away my beauty and my sin. Shrive me, Genyo, shrive me, Holy Man; Let me have peace.*"

"Poor Spirit," said Genyo. "Take my staff and my priestly robe and my begging bowl and set forth upon the long journey of repentance."

Tamamo took the priestly robe and put it upon her; in one hand she took the staff, in the other the bowl. And when she had done this, she vanished for ever from the sight of earthly men.

"O thou, Tathagatha," said Genyo, "and thou, Kwannon, Merciful Lady, make it possible that one day even she may attain Nirvana."

Momotaro

If you'll believe me there was a time when the fairies were none so shy as they are now. That was the time when beasts talked to men, when there were spells and enchantments and magic every day, when there was great store of hidden treasure to be dug up, and adventures for the asking.

At that time, you must know, an old man and an old woman lived alone by themselves. They were good and they were poor and they had no children at all.

One fine day, "What are you doing this morning, good man?" says the old woman.

"Oh," says the old man, "I'm off to the mountains with my billhook to gather a faggot of sticks for our fire. And what are you doing, good wife?"

"Oh," says the old woman, "I'm off to the stream to wash clothes. It's my washing day," she adds.

So the old man went to the mountains and the old woman went to the stream.

Now, while she was washing the clothes, what should she see but a fine ripe peach that came floating down the stream? The peach was big enough, and rosy red on both sides.

"I'm in luck this morning," said the dame, and she pulled the peach to shore with a split bamboo stick.

By- and- by, when her good man came home from the hills, she set the peach before him. "Eat, good man," she said; "this is a lucky peach I found in the stream and brought home for you."

But the old man never got a taste of the peach. And why did he not?

All of a sudden the peach burst in two and there was no stone to it, but a fine boy baby where the stone should have been.

"Mercy me!" says the old woman.

"Mercy me!" says the old man.

The boy baby first ate up one half of the peach and then he ate up the other half. When he had done this he was finer and stronger than ever.

"Momotaro! Momotaro!" cries the old man; "the eldest son of the peach."

"Truth it is indeed," says the old woman; "he was born in a peach."

Both of them took such good care of Momotaro that soon he was the stoutest and bravest boy of all that country- side. He was a credit to them, you may believe. The neighbours nodded their heads and they said, "Momotaro is the fine young man!"

"Mother," says Momotaro one day to the old woman, "make me a good store of *kimi-dango*" (which is the way that they call millet dumplings in those parts).

"What for do you want *kimi- dango?*" says his mother.

"Why," says Momotaro, "I'm going on a journey, or as you may say, an adventure, and I shall be needing the *kimi- dango* on the way."

"Where are you going, Momotaro?" says his mother.

"I'm off to the Ogres' Island," says Momotaro, "to get their treasure, and I should be obliged if you'd let me have the *kimi-dango* as soon as may be," he says.

So they made him the *kimi- dango*, and he put them in a wallet, and he tied the wallet to his girdle and off he set.

"*Sayonara*, and good luck to you, Momotaro!" cried the old man and the old woman.

"*Sayonara! Sayonara!*" cried Momotaro.

He hadn't gone far when he fell in with a monkey.

"Kia! Kia!" says the monkey. "Where are you off to, Momotaro?"

Says Momotaro, "I'm off to the Ogres' Island for an adventure."

"What have you got in the wallet hanging at your girdle?"

"Now you're asking me something," says Momotaro; "sure, I've some of the best millet dumplings in all Japan."

"Give me one," says the monkey, "and I will go with you."

So Momotaro gave a millet dumpling to the monkey, and the two of them jogged on together. They hadn't gone far when they fell in with a pheasant.

"Ken! Ken!" said the pheasant. "Where are you off to, Momotaro?"

Says Momotaro, "I'm off to the Ogres' Island for an adventure."

"What have you got in your wallet, Momotaro?"

"I've got some of the best millet dumplings in all Japan."

"Give me one," says the pheasant, "and I will go with you."

So Momotaro gave a millet dumpling to the pheasant, and the three of them jogged on together.

They hadn't gone far when they fell in with a dog.

"Bow! Wow! Wow!" says the dog. "Where are you off to, Momotaro?"

Says Momotaro, "I'm off to the Ogres' Island."

"What have you got in your wallet, Momotaro?"

"I've got some of the best millet dumplings in all Japan."

"Give me one," says the dog, "and I will go with you."

So Momotaro gave a millet dumpling to the dog, and the four of them jogged on together. By- and- by they came to the Ogres' Island.

"Now, brothers," says Momotaro, "listen to my plan. The pheasant must fly over the castle gate and peck the Ogres. The monkey must climb over the castle wall and pinch the Ogres. The dog and I will break the bolts and bars. He will bite the Ogres, and I will fight the Ogres."

Then there was the great battle.

The pheasant flew over the castle gate: "Ken! Ken! Ken!"

Momotaro broke the bolts and bars, and the dog leapt into the castle courtyard. "Bow! Wow! Wow!"

The brave companions fought till sundown and overcame the Ogres. Those that were left alive they took prisoners and bound with cords- a wicked lot they were.

"Now, brothers," says Momotaro, "bring out the Ogres' treasure."

So they did.

The treasure was worth having, indeed. There were magic jewels there, and caps and coats to make you invisible. There was gold and silver, and jade and coral, and amber and tortoise- shell and mother- of- pearl.

"Here's riches for all," says Momotaro. "Choose, brothers, and take your fill."

"Kia! Kia!" says the monkey. "Thanks, my Lord Momotaro."

"Ken! Ken!" says the pheasant. "Thanks, my Lord Momotaro."

"Bow! Wow! Wow!" says the dog. "Thanks, my dear Lord Momotaro."

The Matsuyama Mirror

A long, long time ago there lived in a quiet spot a young man and his wife. They had one child, a little daughter, whom they both loved with all their hearts. I cannot tell you their names, for they have long since been forgotten; but the name of the place where they lived was Matsuyama, in the Province of Echigo.

It happened once, while the little girl was still a baby, that the father was obliged to go to the great city, the capital of Japan, upon some business. It was too far for the mother and her little baby to go, so he set out alone, after bidding them goodbye and promising to bring them home some pretty present.

The mother had never been farther from home than the next village, and she could not help being a little frightened at the thought of her husband taking such a long journey; and yet she was a little proud too, for he was the first man in all that country- side who had been to the big town where the king and his great lords lived, and where there were so many beautiful and curious things to be seen.

At last the time came when she might expect her husband back, so she dressed the baby in its best clothes, and herself put on a pretty blue dress which she knew her husband liked.

You may fancy how glad this good wife was to see him come home safe and sound, and how the little girl clapped her hands, and laughed with delight when she saw the pretty toys her father had brought for her. He had much to tell of all the wonderful things he had seen upon the journey, and in the town itself.

"I have brought you a very pretty thing," said he to his wife; "it is called a mirror. Look and tell me what you see inside." He gave to her a plain white wooden box, in which, when she had opened it, she found a round piece of metal. One side was white, like frosted silver, and ornamented with raised figures of birds and flowers; the other was bright as the clearest crystal. Into it the young mother looked with delight and astonishment, for, from its depths was looking at her with parted lips and bright eyes, a smiling happy face.

"What do you see?" again asked the husband, pleased at her astonishment and glad to show that he had learned something while he had been away.

"I see a pretty woman looking at me, and she moves her lips as if she was speaking, and- dear me, how odd, she has on a blue dress just like mine!"

"Why, you silly woman, it is your own face that you see!" said the husband, proud of knowing something that his wife didn't know. "That round piece of metal is called a mirror. In the town everybody has one, although we have not seen them in this country- place before."

The wife was charmed with her present, and for a few days could not look into the mirror often enough; for you must remember that as this was the first time she had seen a mirror, so, of course, it was the first time she had ever seen the reflection of her own pretty face. But she considered such a wonderful thing far too precious for everyday use, and soon shut it up in its box again and put it away carefully among her most valued treasures.

Years passed on, and the husband and wife still lived happily. The joy of their life was their little daughter, who grew up the very image of her mother, and who was so dutiful and affectionate that everybody loved her. Mindful of her own little passing vanity on finding herself so lovely, the mother kept the mirror carefully hidden away, fearing that the use of it might breed a spirit of pride in her little girl.

She never spoke of it, and as for the father he had forgotten all about it. So it happened that the daughter grew up as simple as the mother had been, and knew nothing of her own good looks, or of the mirror which would have reflected them.

But by- and- by a terrible misfortune happened to this happy little family. The good, kind mother fell sick; and, although her daughter waited upon her, day and night, with loving care, she got worse and worse, until at last there was no doubt but that she must die.

When she found that she must so soon leave her husband and child, the poor woman felt very sorrowful, grieving for those she was going to leave behind, and most of all for her little daughter.

She called the girl to her and said, "My darling child, you know that I am very sick; soon I must die and leave your dear father and you alone. When I am gone, promise me that you will look into this mirror every night and every morning; there you will see me, and know that I am still watching over you." With these words she took the mirror from its hiding- place and gave it to her daughter. The child promised, with many tears, and so the mother, seeming now calm and resigned, died a short time after.

Now this obedient and dutiful daughter never forgot her mother's last request, but each morning and evening took the mirror from its hiding- place, and looked in it long and earnestly. There she saw the bright and smiling vision of her lost mother. Not pale and sickly as in her last days, but the beautiful young mother of long ago. To her at night she told the story of the trials and difficulties of the day; to her in the morning she looked for sympathy and encouragement in whatever might be in store for her.

So day by day she lived as in her mother's sight, striving still to please her as she had done in her lifetime, and careful always to avoid whatever might pain or grieve her.

Her greatest joy was to be able to look in the mirror and say, "Mother, I have been to-day what you would have me to be."

Seeing her look into the mirror every night and morning without fail, and seem to hold converse with it, her father at length asked her the reason of her strange behaviour. "Father," she said, "I look in the mirror every day to see my dear mother and to talk with her." Then she told him of her mother's dying wish, and how she had never failed to fulfil it. Touched by so much simplicity, and such faithful, loving obedience, the father shed tears of pity

and affection. Nor could he find it in his heart
to tell the child that the image she saw in the
mirror was but the reflection of her own
sweet face, becoming by constant sympathy
and association more and more like her dead
mother's day by day.

Broken Images

Once there lived two brothers who were princes in the land.

The elder brother was a hunter. He loved the deep woods and the chase. He went from dawn to dark with his bow and his arrows. Swiftly he could run; he was strong and bright- eyed. The younger brother was a dreamer; his eyes were gentle. From dawn to dark he would sit with his book or with his thoughts. Sweetly could he sing of love, or of war, or of the green fields, and tell stories of the fairies and of the time of the gods.

Upon a fair day of summer the hunter betook himself very early to the woods, as was his wont. But the dreamer took his book in his hand, and, musing, he wandered by the stream's side, where grew the yellow mimulus.

"It is the fairies' money," he said; "it will buy all the joys of fairyland!" So he went on his way, smiling.

And when he had continued for some time, he came to a holy shrine. And there led to the shrine a hundred steps, moss- grown and grey. Beside the steps were guardian lions, carved in stone. Behind the shrine was Fugi, the Mystic Mountain, white and beautiful, and all the lesser hills rose softly up like prayers.

"O peerless Fugi," said the dreamer, "O passionless wonder mountain! To see thee is to hear sweet music without sound, the blessed harmony of silence."

Then he climbed the steps, moss- grown and grey. And the lions that were carved in stone rose up and followed him, and they came with him to the inner gates of the shrine and stayed there.

In the shrine there was a hush of noonday. The smoke of incense curled and hung upon the air. Dimly shone the gold and the bronze, the lights and the mystic mirrors.

There was a sound of singing in the shrine, and turning, the dreamer saw a man who stood at his right hand. The man was taller than any child of earth. Moreover, his face shone with the glory of a youth that cannot pass away. He held a year- old child upon his arm and hushed it to sleep, singing a strange melody. When the babe fell asleep he was well pleased, and smiled.

"What babe is that?" said the dreamer.

"O dreamer, it is no babe, but a spirit."

"Then, my lord, what are you?" said the dreamer.

"I am Jizo, who guards the souls of little children. It is most pitiful to hear their crying when they come to the sandy river- bed, the *Sai- no- kawara*. O dreamer, they come alone, as needs they must, wailing and wandering, stretching out their pretty hands. They have a task, which is to pile stones for a tower of prayer. But in the night come the *Oni* to throw down the towers and to scatter all the stones. So the children are made afraid, and their labour is lost."

"What then, my lord Jizo?" said the dreamer.

"Why, then I come, for the Great One gives me leave. And I call 'Come hither, wandering souls.' And they fly to me that I may hide them in my long sleeves. I carry them in my arms and on my breast, where they lie light and cold,- as light and cold as the morning mist upon the mountains."

When he had spoken, the year- old child stirred and murmured: so he rocked it, and wandered to and fro in the quiet temple court and hushed it as he went.

So the swift moments flew and the noontide passed away.

Presently there came to the shrine a lady most gentle and beautiful. Grey was her robe, and she had silver sandals on her feet. She said, "I am called The Merciful. For mankind's dear sake, I have refused eternal peace. The Great One has given to me a thousand loving arms, arms of mercy. And my hands are full of gifts. O dreamer, when you dream your dreams you shall see me in my lotus boat when I sail upon the mystic mere."

"Lady, Lady Kwannon ..." said the dreamer.

Then came one clothed in blue, speaking with a sweet, deep, well- known voice.

"I am Benten, the Goddess of the Sea and the Goddess of Song. My dragons are about me and beneath my feet. See their green scales and their opal eyes. Greeting, O dreamer!"

After her there came a band of blooming boys, laughing and holding out their rosy arms. "We are the Sons of the Sea Goddess," they said. "Come, dreamer, come to our cool caves."

The God of Roads came, and his three messengers with him. Three apes were the three messengers. The first ape covered his eyes with his hands, for he could see no evil thing. The second ape covered his ears with his hands, for he could hear no evil thing. The third ape covered his mouth with his hands, for he could speak no evil thing. Then came She, the fearful woman who takes the clothes of the dead who are not able to pay their toll, so that they must stand shivering at the entrance of the mysterious Three Ways. They are unfortunate indeed.

And many and many a vision the dreamer saw in that enchanted shrine.

And dark night fell, with storm and tempest and the sound of rain upon the roof. Yet the dreamer never stirred. Suddenly there was a sound of hurrying feet without. A voice called loud, "My brother, my brother, my brother!..." In sprang the hunter through the golden temple doors.

"Where are you?" he cried, "my brother, my brother!" He had his swinging lantern in his hand and held it high, as he flung his long blown hair back over his shoulder. His face was bright with the rain upon it, his eyes were as keen as an eagle's.

"O brother ..." said the dreamer, and ran to meet him.

"Now the dear gods be thanked that I have you safe and sound," said the hunter. "Half the night I have sought you, wandering in the forest and by the stream's side. I was all to blame for leaving you... my little brother." With that, he took his brother's face between his two warm hands.

But the dreamer sighed, "I have been with the gods all night," he said, "and I think I see them still. The place is holy."

277

Then the hunter flashed his light upon the temple walls, upon the gilding and the bronze.

"I see no gods," he said.

"What see you, brother?"

"I see a row of stones, broken images, grey, with moss- grown feet."

"They are grey because they are sad, they are sad because they are forgotten," said the dreamer.

But the hunter took him by the hand and led him into the night.

The dreamer said, "O brother, how sweet is the scent of the bean fields after the rain."

"Now bind your sandals on," said the hunter, "and I'll run you a race to our home."

The Tongue- cut Sparrow

Once upon a time there was an old man who lived all alone. And there was an old woman who lived all alone. The old man was merry and kind and gentle, with a good word and a smile for all the world. The old woman was sour and sad, as cross a patch as could be found in all the country- side. She grumbled and growled for ever, and would not so much as pass the time of day with respectable folk.

The old man had a pet sparrow that he kept as the apple of his eye. The sparrow could talk and sing and dance and do all manner of tricks, and was very good company. So the old man found when he came home from his work at night. There would be the sparrow twittering on the doorstep, and "Welcome home, master," he would say, his head on one side, as pert and pretty as you please.

One day the old man went off to cut wood in the mountains. The old woman, she stayed at home for it was her washing day. She made some good starch in a bowl and she put it outside her door to cool.

"It will be all ready when I want it," she said to herself. But that's just where she made a mistake. The little sparrow flew over the bamboo fence and lighted on the edge of the starch bowl. And he pecked at the starch with his little beak. He pecked and he pecked till all the starch was gone, and a good meal he made, to be sure.

Then out came the old woman for the starch to starch her clothes.

You may believe she was angry. She caught the little sparrow roughly in her hand, and, alas and alack! she took a sharp, sharp scissors and cut his little tongue. Then she let him go.

Away and away flew the little sparrow, over hill and over dale.

"And a good riddance, too!" said the cruel old woman.

When the old man came home from the mountains he found his pet sparrow gone. And before long he knew all the tale. He lost no time, the good old man; he set out at once on foot, calling "Sparrow, sparrow, where are you, my tongue- cut sparrow?"

Over hill and over dale he went, calling "Sparrow, sparrow, where are you, my tongue- cut sparrow?"

At last and at length he came to the sparrow's house, and the sparrow flew out to greet his master. Then there was a twittering, to be sure. The sparrow called his brothers and sisters and his children and his wife and his mother- in- law and his mother and his grandmother. And they all flew out to do the old man honour. They brought him into the house and they set him down upon mats of silk. Then they spread a great feast; red rice and *daikon* and fish, and who knows what all besides, and the very best *saké* to drink. The sparrow waited upon the good old man, and his brothers and sisters and his children and his wife and his mother- in- law and his mother and his grandmother with him.

After supper the sparrow danced, whilst his grandmother played the *samisen* and the good old man beat time.

It was a merry evening.

At last, "All good things come to an end," says the old man; "I fear 'tis late and high time I was getting home."

"Not without a little present," says the sparrow.

"Ah, sparrow dear," says the old man, "I'd sooner have yourself than any present."

But the sparrow shook his head.

Presently they brought in two wicker baskets.

"One of them is heavy," says the sparrow, "and the other is light. Say, master, will you take the heavy basket or the light?"

"I'm not so young as I once was," says the good old man. "Thanking you kindly, I'd sooner have the light basket; it will suit me better to carry- that is, if it's the same to you," he says.

So he went home with the light basket. When he opened it, wonderful to tell, it was full of gold and silver and tortoise- shell and coral and jade and fine rolls of silk. So the good old man was rich for life.

Now, when the bad old woman heard tell of all this, she tied on her sandals and kilted her skirts and took a stout stick in her hand. Over hill and over dale she went, and took the straight road to the sparrow's house. There was the sparrow, and there were his brothers and sisters and children and his wife and his mother and his mother- in- law and his grandmother. They were not too pleased to see the bad old woman, but they couldn't do less than ask her in as she'd come so far. They gave her red rice and white rice and *daikon* and fish, and who knows what besides, and she gobbled it up in a twinkling, and drank a good cup of *saké*. Then up she got. "I can't waste any more time here," she says, "so you'd best bring out your presents."

They brought in two wicker baskets.

"One of them is heavy," says the sparrow, "and the other is light. Say, mistress, will you take the heavy basket or the light?"

"I'll take the heavy one," says the old woman, quick as a thought. So she heaved it up on her back and off she set. Sure enough it was as heavy as lead.

When she was gone, Lord! how the sparrows did laugh!

No sooner did she reach home than she undid the cords of the basket.

"Now for the gold and silver," she said, and smiled- though she hadn't smiled for a twelve- month. And she lifted up the lid.

"*Ai! Ai! Kowai! Obaké da! Obaké!*" she screeched.

The basket was full of ugly imps and elves and pixies and demons and devils. Out they came to tease the old woman, to pull her and to poke her, to push her and to pinch her. She had the fine fright of her life, I warrant you.

The Nurse

Idé the *samurai* was wedded to a fair wife and had an only child, a boy called Fugiwaka. Idé was a mighty man of war, and as often as not he was away from home upon the business of his liege lord. So the child Fugiwaka was reared by his mother and by the faithful woman, his nurse. Matsu was her name, which is, in the speech of the country, the Pine Tree. And even as the pine tree, strong and evergreen, was she, unchanging and enduring.

In the house of Idé there was a very precious sword. Aforetime a hero of Idé's clan slew eight- and- forty of his enemies with this sword in one battle. The sword was Idé's most sacred treasure. He kept it laid away in a safe place with his household gods.

Morning and evening the child Fugiwaka came to make salutations before the household gods, and to reverence the glorious memory of his ancestors. And Matsu, the nurse, knelt by his side.

Morning and evening, "Show me the sword, O Matsu, my nurse," said Fugiwaka.

And O Matsu made answer, "Of a surety, my lord, I will show it to you."

Then she brought the sword from its place, wrapped in a covering of red and gold brocade. And she drew off the covering and she took the sword from its golden sheath and displayed the bright steel to Fugiwaka. And the child made obeisance till his forehead touched the mats.

At bedtime O Matsu sang songs and lullabies. She sang this song:

"Sleep, my little child, sweetly sleep- Would you know the secret, The secret of the hare o Nennin Yama? Sleep, my little child, sweetly sleep- You shall know the secret. Oh, the august hare of Nennin Yama, How augustly long are his ears! Why should this be, oh, best beloved? You shall know the secret. His mother ate the bamboo seed. Hush! Hush! His mother ate the loquat seed. Hush! Hush! Sleep, my little child, sweetly sleep- Now you know the secret."

Then O Matsu said, "Will you sleep now, my lord Fugiwaka?"

And the child answered, "I will sleep now, O Matsu."

"Listen, my lord," she said, "and, sleeping or waking, remember. The sword is your treasure. The sword is your trust. The sword is your fortune. Cherish it, guard it, keep it."

"Sleeping or waking, I will remember," said Fugiwaka.

Now in an evil day the mother of Fugiwaka fell sick and died. And there was mourning in the house of Idé. Howbeit, when years were past, the *samurai* took another bride, and he had a son by her and called him Goro. And after this Idé himself was slain in an ambush, and his retainers brought his body home and laid him with his fathers.

Fugiwaka was chief of the House of Idé. But the Lady Sadako, his stepmother, was ill-pleased. Black mischief stirred in her heart; she bent her brows and she brooded as she went her ways, bearing her babe in her arms. At night she tossed upon her bed.

"My child is a beggar," she said. "Fugiwaka is chief of the House of Idé. Evil fortune betide him! It is too much," said the proud lady. "I will not brook it; my child a beggar! I would rather strangle him with my hands...." Thus she spoke and tossed upon her bed, thinking of a plan.

When Fugiwaka was fifteen years old she turned him out of the house with a poor garment upon his back, barefooted, with never a bite nor a sup nor a gold piece to see him on his way.

"Ah, lady mother," he said, "you use me ill. Why do you take my birthright?"

"I know nought of birthrights," she said. "Go, make your own fortune if you can. Your brother Goro is chief of the House of Idé."

With that she bade them shut the door in his face.

Fugiwaka departed sorrowfully, and at the cross- roads O Matsu, his nurse, met him. She had made herself ready for a journey: her robe was kilted, she had a staff in her hand and sandals on her feet.

"My lord," she said, "I am come to follow you to the world's end."

Then Fugiwaka wept and laid his head upon the woman's breast.

"Ah," he said, "my nurse, my nurse! And," he said, "what of my father's sword? I have lost the precious sword of Idé. The sword is my treasure, the sword is my trust, the sword is my fortune. I am bound to cherish it, to guard it, to keep it. But now I have lost it. Woe is me! I am undone, and so is all the House of Idé!"

"Oh, say not so, my lord," said O Matsu. "Here is gold; go you your way and I will return and guard the sword of Idé."

So Fugiwaka went his way with the gold that his nurse gave him.

As for O Matsu, she went straightway and took the sword from its place where it lay with the household gods, and she buried it deep in the ground until such time as she might bear it in safety to her young lord.

But soon the Lady Sadako became aware that the sacred sword was gone.

"It is the nurse!" she cried. "The nurse has stolen it.... Some of you bring her to me."

Then the Lady Sadako's people laid their hands roughly upon O Matsu and brought her before their mistress. But for all they could do O Matsu's lips were sealed. She spoke never a word, neither could the Lady Sadako find out where the sword was. She pressed her thin lips together.

"The woman is obstinate," she said. "No matter; for such a fault I know the sovereign cure."

So she locked O Matsu in a dark dungeon and gave her neither food nor drink. Every day the Lady Sadako went to the door of the dark dungeon.

"Well," she said, "where is the sword of Idé? Will you say?"

But O Matsu answered not a word.

Howbeit she wept and sighed to herself in the darkness- "Alas! Alas! never alive may I come to my young lord. Yet he must have the sword of Idé, and I shall find a way."

Now after seven days the Lady Sadako sat in the garden- house to cool herself, for it was summer. The time was evening. Presently she saw a woman that came towards her through the garden flowers and trees. Frail and slender was the woman; as she came her body swayed and her slow steps faltered.

"Why, this is strange!" said the Lady Sadako. "Here is O Matsu, that was locked in the dark dungeon." And she sat still, watching.

But O Matsu went to the place where she had buried the sword and scratched at the ground with her fingers. There she was, weeping and moaning and dragging at the earth. The stones cut her hands and they bled. Still she tore away the earth and found the sword at last. It was in its wrapping of gold and scarlet, and she clasped it to her bosom with a loud cry.

"Woman, I have you now," shrieked the Lady Sadako, "and the sword of Idé as well!" And she leaped from the garden- house and ran at full speed. She stretched forth her hand to catch O Matsu by the sleeve, but did not have her or the sword either, for both of them were gone in a flash, and the lady beat the empty air. Swiftly she sped to the dark dungeon, and as she went she called her people to bring torches. There lay the body of poor O Matsu, cold and dead upon the dungeon floor.

"Send me the Wise Woman," said the Lady Sadako.

So they sent for the Wise Woman. And the Lady Sadako asked, "How long has she been dead?"

The Wise Woman said, "She was starved to death; she has been dead two days. It were well you gave her fit burial; she was a good soul."

As for the sword of Idé, it was not found.

Fugiwaka tossed to and fro upon his lowly bed in a wayside tavern. And it seemed to him that his nurse came to him and knelt by his side. Then he was soothed.

O Matsu said, "Will you sleep now, my lord Fugiwaka?"

And he answered, "I will sleep now, O Matsu."

"Listen, my lord," she said, "and, sleeping or waking, remember. The sword is your treasure. The sword is your trust. The sword is your fortune. Cherish it, guard it, keep it."

The sword was in its wrapping of gold and scarlet, and she laid it by Fugiwaka's side. The boy turned over to sleep, and his hand clasped the sword of Idé.

"Waking or sleeping," he said, "I will remember."

The Beautiful Dancer of Yedo

This is the tale of Sakura- ko, Flower of the Cherry, who was the beautiful dancer of Yedo.

She was a *geisha*, born a *samurai's* daughter, that sold herself into bondage after her father died, so that her mother might have food to eat. Ah, the pity of it! The money that bought her was called *Namida no Kané*, that is "the money of tears."

She dwelt in the narrow street of the *geisha*, where the red and white lanterns swing and the plum trees flourish by the low eves. The street of the *geisha* is full of music, for they play the *samisen* there all day long.

Sakura- ko played it too; indeed she was skilful in every lovely art. She played the *samisen*, the *kotto*, the *biwa*, and the small hand- drum. She could make songs and sing them. Her eyes were long, her hair was black, her hands were white. Her beauty was wonderful, and wonderful her power to please. From dawn to dusk, and from dusk to dawn she could go smiling and hide her heart. In the cool of the day she would stand upon the gallery of her mistress's house, and muse as she stood and looked down into the street of the *geisha*. And the folk that passed that way said to one another, "See, yonder stands Sakura- ko, Flower of the Cherry, the beautiful dancer of Yedo, the *geisha* without peer."

But Sakura- ko looked down and mused and said, "Little narrow street of the *geisha*, paved with bitterness and broken hearts, your houses are full of vain hopes and vain regrets; youth and love and grief dwell here. The flowers in your gardens are watered with tears."

The gentlemen of Yedo must needs have their pleasure, so Sakura- ko served at feasts every night. They whitened her cheeks and her forehead, and gilded her lips with *beni*. She wore silk attires, gold and purple and grey and green and black, *obi* of brocade magnificently tied. Her hair was pinned with coral and jade, fastened with combs of gold lacquer and tortoise- shell. She poured *saké*, she made merry with the good company. More than this, she danced.

Three poets sang of her dancing. One said, "She is lighter than the rainbow- tinted dragonfly."

And another said, "She moves like the mist of the morning when the bright sun shines."

And the third said, "She is like the shadow in the river of the waving willow- branch."

But it is time to tell of her three lovers.

The first lover was neither old nor young. He was passing rich, and a great man in Yedo. He sent his servant to the street of the *geisha* with money in his girdle. Sakura- ko shut the door in his face.

"You are wrong, fellow," she said, "you have lost your way. You should have gone to the street of the toy- shops and bought your master a doll; let him know there are no dolls here."

After this the master came himself. "Come to me, O Flower of the Cherry," he said, "for I must have you."

"*Must?*" she said, and looked down with her long eyes.

"Aye," he said, "must is the word, O Flower of the Cherry."

"What will you give me?" she said.

"Fine attires, silk and brocade, a house, white mats and cool galleries; servants to wait on you, gold hairpins- what you will."

"What do I give you?" she said.

"Yourself, just that, O Flower of the Cherry."

"Body and soul?" she said.

And he answered her, "Body and soul."

"Now, fare you well," she said, "I have a fancy to remain a *geisha*. It is a merry life," she said, and she laughed.

So that was the end of the first lover.

The second lover was old. To be old and wise is very well, but he was old and foolish. "Sakura- ko," he cried, "ah, cruel one, I am mad for love of you!"

"My lord," she said, "I can easily believe it."

He said, "I am not so very old."

"By the divine compassion of the gods," she told him, "you may yet have time to prepare for your end. Go home and read the good law." But the old lover would hear nothing of her counsel. Instead, he bade her to his house by night to a great feast which he had prepared for her. And when they had made an end of the feast she danced before him wearing scarlet *hakama* and a robe of gold brocade. After the dancing he made her sit beside him and he called for wine, that they might drink together. And the *geisha* who poured the *saké* was called Silver Wave.

When they had drunk together, Sakura- ko and her old lover, he drew her to him and cried:

"Come, my love, my bride, you are mine for the time of many existences; there was poison in the cup. Be not afraid, for we shall die together. Come with me to the Meido."

But Sakura- ko said, "My sister, the Silver Wave, and I are not children, neither are we old and foolish to be deceived. I drank no *saké* and no poison. My sister, the Silver Wave, poured fresh tea in my cup. Howbeit I am sorry for you, and so I will stay with you till you die."

He died in her arms and was fain to take his way alone to the Meido.

"Alas! alas!" cried the Flower of the Cherry. But her sister, Silver Wave, gave her counsel thus: "Keep your tears, you will yet have cause for weeping. Waste not grief for such as he."

And that was the end of the second lover.

The third lover was young and brave and gay. Impetuous he was, and beautiful. He first set eyes on the Flower of the Cherry at a festival in his father's house. Afterwards he went to seek her out in the street of the *geisha*. He found her as she leaned against the gallery railing of her mistress's house.

She looked down into the street of the *geisha* and sang this song:

"My mother bade me spin fine thread Out of the yellow sea sand- A hard task, a hard task. May the dear gods speed me! My father gave me a basket of

reeds; He said, 'Draw water from the spring And carry it a mile'- A hard task, a hard task. May the dear gods speed me! My heart would remember, My heart must forget; Forget, my heart, forget- A hard task, a hard task. May the dear gods speed me!'

When she had made an end of singing, the lover saw that her eyes were full of tears.

"Do you remember me," he said, "O Flower of the Cherry? I saw you last night at my father's house."

"Aye, my young lord," she answered him, "I remember you very well."

He said, "I am not so very young. And I love you, O Flower of the Cherry. Be gentle, hear me, be free, be my dear wife."

At this she flushed neck and chin, cheeks and forehead.

"My dear," said the young man, "now you are Flower of the Cherry indeed."

"Child," she said, "go home and think of me no more. I am too old for such as you."

"Old!" he said; "why, there lies not a year between us!"

"No, not a year- no year, but an eternity," said Flower of the Cherry. "Think no more of me," she said; but the lover thought of nothing else. His young blood was on fire. He could not eat, nor drink, nor sleep. He pined and grew pale, he wandered day and night, his heart heavy with longing. He lived in torment; weak he grew, and weaker. One night he fell fainting at the entrance of the street of the *geisha*. Sakura- ko came home at dawn from a festival in a great house. There she found him. She said no word, but she bore him to his house outside Yedo, and stayed with him there full three moons. And after that time he was nursed back to ruddy health. Swiftly, swiftly, the glad days sped by for both of them.

"This is the happy time of all my life. I thank the dear gods," said Flower of the Cherry one evening.

"My dear," the young man bade her, "fetch hither your *samisen* and let me hear you sing."

So she did. She said, "I shall sing you a song you have heard already."

"My mother bade me spin fine thread Out of the yellow sea sand- A hard task, a hard task. May the dear gods speed me! My father gave me a basket of reeds; He said, 'Draw water from the spring And carry it a mile'- A hard task, a hard task. May the dear gods speed me! My heart would remember, My heart must forget; Forget, my heart, forget- A hard task, a hard task. May the dear gods speed me!"

"Sweet," he said, "what does this song mean, and why do you sing it?"

She answered, "My lord, it means that I must leave you, and therefore do I sing it. I must forget you; you must forget me. That is my desire."

He said, "I will never forget you, not in a thousand existences."

She smiled, "Pray the gods you may wed a sweet wife and have children."

He cried, "No wife but you, and no children but yours, O Flower of the Cherry."

"The gods forbid, my dear, my dear. All the world lies between us."

The next day she was gone. High and low the lover wandered, weeping and lamenting and seeking her both near and far. It was all in vain, for he found her not. The city of Yedo knew her no more- Sakura- ko, the beautiful dancer.

And her lover mourned many many days. Howbeit at last he was comforted, and they found for him a very sweet fair lady whom he took to wife willingly enough, and soon she bore him a son. And he was glad, for time dries all tears.

Now when the boy was five years old he sat in the gate of his father's house. And it chanced that a wandering nun came that way begging for alms. The servants of the house brought rice and would have put it into her begging bowl, but the child said, "Let me give."

So he did as he would.

As he filled the begging bowl and patted down the rice with a wooden spoon and laughed, the nun caught him by the sleeve and held him and looked into his eyes.

"Holy nun, why do you look at me so?" cried the child.

She said, "Because I once had a little boy like you, and I went away and left him."

"Poor little boy!" said the child.

"It was better for him, my dear, my dear—far, far better."

And when she had said this, she went her way.

Hana- Saka- Jiji

In the early days there lived a good old couple. All their lives long they had been honest and hard- working, but they had always been poor. Now in their old age it was all they could do to make both ends meet, the poor old creatures.

But they did not complain, not a bit of it. They were merry as the day is long. If they ever went to bed cold or hungry they said nothing about it, and if they had bite or sup in the house you may be sure they shared it with their dog, for they were very fond of him. He was faithful, good, and clever. One evening the old man and the old woman went out to do a bit of digging in their garden, and the dog went with them.

While they were working the dog was sniffing the ground, and presently he began to scratch up the earth with his paws.

"What can the dog be about now?" says the old woman.

"Oh, just nothing at all," says the old man; "he's playing."

"It's more than playing," says the old woman. "It's my belief he's found something worth having."

So off she went to see what the dog would be at, and the old man followed her and leaned on his spade. Sure enough the dog had dug a pretty big hole by this time, and he went on scratching with his paws for dear life and barking short and sharp. The old man helped with his spade, and before long they came on a big box of hidden treasure, silver and gold and jewels and rich stuffs.

It is easy to believe that the good old couple were glad. They patted their clever dog, and he jumped up and licked their faces. After this they carried the treasure into the house. The dog ran to and fro and barked.

Now, next door to the good old couple lived another old couple, not so good as they, but envious and discontented. When the dog found the hidden treasure they looked through a hole in the bamboo hedge and saw the whole affair. Do you think they were pleased? Why, not a bit of it. They were so angry and envious that they could get no pleasure by day nor rest at night.

At last the bad old man came to the good old man.

"I've come to ask for the loan of your dog," he says.

"With all my heart," says the good old man; "take him and welcome."

So the bad old man took the dog and brought him to their best room. And the bad old man and his wife put a supper, of all manner of fine things to eat, before the dog, and bade him fall to.

"Honourable Dog," they said, "you are good and wise, eat and afterwards find us treasure."

But the dog would not eat.

"All the more left for us," said the greedy old couple, and they ate up the dog's supper in a twinkling. Then they tied a string round his neck and dragged him into the garden to find treasure. But never a morsel of treasure did he find, nor a glint of gold, nor a shred of rich stuff.

"The devil's in the beast," cries the bad old man, and he beat the dog with a big stick. Then the dog began to scratch up the earth with his paws.

"Oho! Oho!" says the bad old man to his wife, "now for the treasure."

But was it treasure that the dog dug up? Not a bit of it. It was a heap of loathly rubbish, too bad to tell of. But they say it smelt most vilely and the bad old couple were fain to run away, hiding their noses with their sleeves.

"Arah, arah!" they cried, "the dog has deceived us." And that very night they killed the poor dog and buried him at the foot of a tall pine tree.

Alack for the good old man and the good old woman when they heard the dog was gone! It was they that wept the bitter tears. They pulled flowers and strewed them on the poor dog's grave. They burned incense and they spread out good things to eat, and the vapour that rose from them comforted the poor dog's spirit.

Then the good old man cut down the pine tree, and made a mortar of its wood. He put rice in the mortar and pounded the rice with a pestle.

"Wonder of wonders," cried the old woman, who was looking on, "wonder of wonders, good man, our rice is all turned into broad gold pieces!"

So it was sure enough.

Presently, in comes the bad old man to ask for the loan of the mortar.

"For I'm needing a mortar something very special," says he.

"Take it," says the good old man; "I'm sure you're welcome."

So the bad old man took away the mortar under his arm, and when he had got it home he filled it with rice in a twinkling. And he pounded away at it for dear life's sake.

"Do you see any gold coming?" he says to his wife, who was looking on.

"Never a bit," she says, "but the rice looks queer."

Queer enough it was, mildewed and rotten, no use to man or beast.

"Arah, arah!" they cried, "the mortar has deceived us." And they didn't let the grass grow under their feet, but lit a fire and burnt the mortar.

Now the good old couple had lost their fairy mortar. But they never said a word, the patient old folk. The good old man took some of the ashes of the mortar and went his way.

Now it was mid- winter time, and all the trees were bare. There was not a flower to be seen, nor yet a little green leaf.

What does the good old man do but climb into a cherry tree and scatter a handful of his ashes over the branches? In a moment the tree was covered with blossoms.

"It will do," says the good old man, and down he gets from the tree and off he sets for the Prince's palace, where he knocks at the gate as bold as brass.

"Who are you?" they ask him.

"I am *Hana- saka- jiji*," says the old man, "the man who makes dead trees to blossom; my business is with the Prince."

Mighty pleased the Prince was when he saw his cherry trees and his peach trees and his plum trees rush into blossom.

"Why," he said, "it is mid- winter, and we have the joys of spring." And he called forth his lady wife and her maidens and all his own retainers to see the work of *Hana- saka- jiji*. At last he sent the old man home with a passing rich reward.

Now what of the bad old couple? Were they content to let well alone? Oh no.

They gathered together all the ashes that were left, and when they had put them in a basket they went about the town crying:

"We are the *Hana- saka- jiji*. We can make dead trees blossom."

Presently out comes the Prince and all his company to see the show. And the bad old man climbs up into a tree forthwith and scatters his ashes.

But the tree never blossomed, never a bit. The ashes flew into the Prince's eyes, and the Prince flew into a rage. There was a pretty to- do. The bad old couple were caught and well beaten. Sad and sorry they crept home at night. It is to be hoped that they mended their ways. Howbeit the good people, their neighbours, grew rich and lived happy all their days.

The Moon Maiden

There was an old bamboo cutter called Také Tori. He was an honest old man, very poor and hard- working, and he lived with his good old wife in a cottage on the hills. Children they had none, and little comfort in their old age, poor souls.

Také Tori rose early upon a summer morning, and went forth to cut bamboos as was his wont, for he sold them for a fair price in the town, and thus he gained his humble living.

Up the steep hillside he went, and came to the bamboo grove quite wearied out. He took his blue *tenegui* and wiped his forehead, "Alack for my old bones!" he said. "I am not so young as I once was, nor the good wife either, and there's no chick nor child to help us in our old age, more's the pity." He sighed as he got to work, poor Také Tori.

Soon he saw a bright light shining among the green stems of the bamboos.

"What is this?" said Také Tori, for as a rule it was dim and shady enough in the bamboo grove. "Is it the sun?" said Také Tori. "No, that cannot well be, for it comes from the ground." Very soon he pushed his way through the bamboo stems to see what the bright light came from. Sure enough it came from the root of a great big green bamboo. Také Tori took his axe and cut down the great big green bamboo, and there was a fine shining green jewel, the size of his two fists.

"Wonder of wonders!" cried Také Tori. "Wonder of wonders! For five- and- thirty years I've cut bamboo. This is the very first time I've found a great big green jewel at the root of one of them." With that he takes up the jewel in his hands, and as soon as he does that, it bursts in two with a loud noise, if you'll believe it, and out of it came a young person and stood on Také Tori's hand.

You must understand the young person was small but very beautiful. She was dressed all in green silk.

"Greetings to you, Také Tori," she says, as easy as you please.

"Mercy me!" says Také Tori. "Thank you kindly. I suppose, now, you'll be a fairy," he says, "if I'm not making too bold in asking?"

"You're right," she says, "it's a fairy I am, and I'm come to live with you and your good wife for a little."

"Well, now," says Také Tori, "begging your pardon, we're very poor. Our cottage is good enough, but I'm afraid there'd be no comforts for a lady like you."

"Where's the big green jewel?" says the fairy.

Také Tori picks up the two halves. "Why, it's full of gold pieces," he says.

"That will do to go on with," says the fairy; "and now, Také Tori, let us make for home."

Home they went. "Wife! wife!" cried Také Tori, "here's a fairy come to live with us, and she has brought us a shining jewel as big as a persimmon, full of gold pieces."

The good wife came running to the door. She could hardly believe her eyes.

"What is this," she said, "about a persimmon and gold pieces? Persimmons I have seen often enough- moreover, it is the season- but gold pieces are hard to come by."

"Let be, woman," said Také Tori, "you are dull." And he brought the fairy into the house.

Wondrous fast the fairy grew. Before many days were gone she was a fine tall maiden, as fresh and as fair as the morning, as bright as the noonday, as sweet and still as the evening, and as deep as the night. Také Tori called her the Lady Beaming Bright, because she had come out of the shining jewel.

Take Tori had the gold pieces out of the jewel every day. He grew rich, and spent his money like a man, but there was always plenty and to spare. He built him a fine house, he had servants to wait on him. The Lady Beaming Bright was lodged like an empress. Her beauty was famed both near and far, and scores of lovers came to seek her hand.

But she would have none of them. "Také Tori and the dear good wife are my true lovers," she said; "I will live with them and be their daughter."

So three happy years went by; and in the third year the Mikado himself came to woo the Lady Beaming Bright. He was the brave lover, indeed.

"Lady," he said, "I bow before you, my soul salutes you. Sweet lady, be my Queen."

Then the Lady Beaming Bright sighed and great tears stood in her eyes, and she hid her face with her sleeve.

"Lord, I cannot," she said.

"Cannot?" said the Mikado; "and why not, O dear Lady Beaming Bright?"

"Wait and see, lord," she said.

Now about the seventh month she grew very sorrowful, and would go abroad no more, but was for long upon the garden gallery of Také Tori's house. There she sat in the daytime and brooded. There she sat at night and gazed upon the moon and the stars. There she was one fine night when the moon was at its full. Her maidens were with her, and Také Tori and the good wife, and the Mikado, her brave lover.

"How bright the moon shines!" said Také Tori.

"Truly," said the good wife, "it is like a brass saucepan well scoured."

"See how pale and wan it is," said the Mikado; "it is like a sad despairing lover."

"How long and bright a beam!" quoth Také Tori. "It is like a highway from the moon reaching to this garden gallery."

"O dear foster- father," cried the Lady Beaming Bright. "You speak truth, it is a highway indeed. And along the highway come countless heavenly beings swiftly, swiftly, to bear me home. My father is the King of the Moon. I disobeyed his behest. He sent me to earth three years to dwell in exile. The three years are past and I go to mine own country. Ah, I am sad at parting."

"The mist descends," said Také Tori.

"Nay," said the Mikado, "it is the cohorts of the King of the Moon."

Down they came in their hundreds and their thousands, bearing torches. Silently they came, and lighted round about the garden gallery. The chief among them brought a heavenly feather robe. Up rose the Lady Beaming Bright and put the robe upon her.

"Farewell, Také Tori," she said, "farewell, dear foster- mother, I leave you my jewel for a remembrance.... As for you, my lord, I would you might come with me- but there is no feather robe for you. I leave you a phial of the pure elixir of life. Drink, my lord, and be even as the Immortals."

Then she spread her bright wings and the cohorts of Heaven closed about her. Together they passed up the highway to the moon, and were no more seen.

The Mikado took the elixir of life in his hand, and he went to the top of the highest mountain in that country. And he made a great fire to consume the elixir of life, for he said, "Of what profit shall it be to me to live for ever, being parted from the Lady Beaming Bright?"

So the elixir of life was consumed, and its blue vapour floated up to Heaven. And the Mikado said, "Let my message float up with the vapour and reach the ears of my Lady Beaming Bright."

Karma

The young man, Ito Tatewaki, was returning homeward after a journey which he had taken to the city of Kioto. He made his way alone and on foot, and he went with his eyes bent upon the ground, for cares weighed him down and his mind was full of the business which had taken him to Kioto. Night found him upon a lonely road leading across a wild moor. Upon the moor were rocks and stones, with an abundance of flowers, for it was summer time, and here and there grew a dark pine tree, with gnarled trunk and crooked boughs.

Tatewaki looked up and beheld the figure of a woman before him in the way. It was a slender girl dressed in a simple gown of blue cotton. Lightly she went along the lonely road in the deepening twilight.

"I should say she was the serving- maid of some gentle lady," Tatewaki said to himself. "The way is solitary and the time is dreary for such a child as she."

So the young man quickened his pace and came up with the maiden. "Child," he said very gently, "since we tread the same lonely road let us be fellow- travellers, for now the twilight passes and it will soon be dark."

The pretty maiden turned to him with bright eyes and smiling lips.

"Sir," she said, "my mistress will be glad indeed."

"Your mistress?" said Tatewaki.

"Why, sir, of a surety she will be glad because you are come."

"Because I am come?"

"Indeed, and indeed the time has been long," said the serving- maid; "but now she will think no more of that."

"Will she not?" said Tatewaki. And on he went by the maiden's side, walking as one in a dream.

Presently the two of them came to a little house, not far from the roadside. Before the house was a small fair garden, with a stream running through it and a stone bridge. About the house and the garden there was a bamboo fence, and in the fence a wicket- gate.

"Here dwells my mistress," said the serving- maid. And they went into the garden through the wicket- gate.

Now Tatewaki came to the threshold of the house. He saw a lady standing upon the threshold waiting.

She said, "You have come at last, my lord, to give me comfort."

And he answered, "I have come."

When he had said this he knew that he loved the lady, and had loved her since love was.

"O love, love," he murmured, "time is not for such as we."

Then she took him by the hand, and they went into the house together and into a room with white mats and a round latticed window.

Before the window there stood a lily in a vessel of water.

Here the two held converse together.

And after some time there was an old ancient woman that came with *saké* in a silver flagon; and she brought silver drinking- cups and all things needful. And Tatewaki and the lady drank the "Three Times Three" together. When they had done this the lady said, "Love, let us go out into the shine of the moon. See, the night is as green as an emerald...."

So they went and left the house and the small fair garden behind them. Or ever they had closed the wicket- gate the house and the garden and the wicket- gate itself all faded away, dissolving in a faint mist, and not a sign of them was left.

"Alas! what is this?" cried Tatewaki.

"Let be, dear love," said the lady, and smiled; "they pass, for we have no more need of them."

Then Tatewaki saw that he was alone with the lady upon the wild moor. And the tall lilies grew about them in a ring. So they stood the live- long night, not touching one another but looking into each other's eyes most steadfastly. When dawn came, the lady stirred and gave one deep sigh.

Tatewaki said, "Lady, why do you sigh?"

And when he asked her this, she unclasped her girdle, which was fashioned after the form of a golden scaled dragon with translucent eyes. And she took the girdle and wound it nine times about her love's arm, and she said, "O love, we part: these are the years until we meet again." So she touched the golden circles on his arm.

Then Tatewaki cried aloud, "O love, who are you? Tell me your name...."

She said, "O love, what have we to do with names, you and I?... I go to my people upon the plains. Do not seek for me there.... Wait for me."

And when the lady had spoken she faded slowly and grew ethereal, like a mist. And Tatewaki cast himself upon the ground and put out his hand to hold her sleeve. But he could not stay her. And his hand grew cold and he lay still as one dead, all in the grey dawn.

When the sun was up he arose.

"The plains," he said, "the low plains... there will I find her." So, with the golden token wound about his arm, fleetly he sped down, down to the plains. He came to the broad river, where he saw folk standing on the green banks. And on the river there floated boats of fresh flowers, the red dianthus and the campanula, golden rod and meadow-sweet. And the people upon the river banks called to Tatewaki:

"Stay with us. Last night was the Night of Souls. They came to earth and wandered where they would, the kind wind carried them. To-day they return to Yomi. They go in their boats of flowers, the river bears them. Stay with us and bid the departing Souls good speed."

And Tatewaki cried, "May the Souls have sweet passage.... I cannot stay."

So he came to the plains at last, but did not find his lady. Nothing at all did he find, but a wilderness of ancient graves, with nettles overgrown and the waving green grass.

So Tatewaki went to his own place, and for nine long years he lived a lonely man. The happiness of home and little children he never knew.

"Ah, love," he said, "not patiently, not patiently, I wait for you.... Love, delay not your coming."

And when the nine years were past he was in his garden upon the Night of Souls. And looking up he saw a woman that came towards him, threading her way through the paths of the garden. Lightly she came; she was a slender girl, dressed in a simple gown of blue cotton. Tatewaki stood up and spoke:

"Child," he said very gently, "since we tread the same lonely road let us be fellow-travellers, for now the twilight passes and it will soon be dark."

The maid turned to him with bright eyes and smiling lips:

"Sir," she said, "my mistress will be glad indeed."

"Will she be glad?" said Tatewaki.

"The time has been long."

"Long and very weary," said Tatewaki.

"But now you will think no more of that...."

"Take me to your mistress," said Tatewaki. "Guide me, for I cannot see any more. Hold me, for my limbs fail. Do not leave go my hand, for I am afraid. Take me to your mistress," said Tatewaki.

In the morning his servants found him cold and dead, quietly lying in the shade of the garden trees.

The Sad Story of the Yaoya's Daughter

There was a wandering ballad- singer who came to a great house in Yedo where they wished to be entertained.

"Will you have a dance or a song?" said the ballad- singer; "or shall I tell you a story?" The people of the house bade him tell a story.

"Shall it be a tale of love or a tale of war?" said the ballad- singer.

"Oh, a tale of love," they said.

"Will you have a sad tale or a merry?" asked the ballad- singer.

They were all agreed that they would hear a sad tale.

"Well, then," said the ballad- singer, "listen, and I will tell you the sad story of the Yaoya's daughter."

So he told this tale.

The Yaoya was a poor hard- working man, but his daughter was the sweetest thing in Yedo. You must know she was one of the five beauties of the city, that grew like five cherry- trees in the time of the spring blossoming.

In autumn the hunters lure the wild deer with the sound of the flute. The deer are

:ived, for they believe that they hear the voices of their mates. So are they trapped and slain. For like calls to like. Youth calls to youth, beauty to beauty, love to love. This is law, and this law was the undoing of the Yaoya's daughter.

When there was a great fire in Yedo, so great that more than the half of the city was burned, the Yaoya's house was ruined also. And the Yaoya and his wife and his daughter had no roof over them, nor anywhere to lay their heads. So they went to a Buddhist temple for shelter and stayed there many days, till their house should be rebuilt. Ah me, for the Yaoya's daughter! Every morning at sunrise she bathed in the spring of clean water that was near the temple. Her eyes were bright and her cheeks ruddy. Then she would put on her blue gown and sit by the water- side to comb her long hair. She was a sweet and slender thing, scarce fifteen years old. Her name was O Schichi.

"Sweep the temple and the temple courts," her father bade her. "'Tis well we should do so much for the good priests who give us shelter." So O Schichi took the broom and swept. And as she laboured she sang merrily, and the grey precincts of the temple grew bright.

Now there was a young acolyte who served in the holy place. Gentle he was and beautiful. Not a day passed but he heard the singing of O Schichi; not a day passed but he set eyes upon her, going her ways, so light and slender, in the ancient courts of the temple.

It was not long before he loved her. Youth calls to youth, beauty to beauty, love to love. It was not long before she loved him.

Secretly they met together in the temple grove. Hand in hand they went, her head against his arm.

"Ah," she cried, "that such a thing should be! I am happy and unhappy. Why do I love you, my own?"

"Because of the power of Karma," said the acolyte. "Nevertheless, we sin, O heart's desire, grievously we sin, and I know not what may come of it."

"Alas," she said, "will the gods be angry with us, and we so young?"

"I cannot tell," he said; "but I am afraid."

Then the two of them clung together, trembling and weeping. But they pledged themselves to each other for the space of many existences.

The Yaoya had his dwelling in the quarter of the city called Honjo, and presently his house was rebuilt which had been destroyed by the fire. He and his wife were glad, for they said, "Now we shall go home."

O Schichi hid her face with her sleeve and wept bitter tears.

"Child, what ails you?" said her mother.

O Schichi wept. "Oh! oh! oh!" she cried, and swayed herself to and fro.

"Why, maid, what is it?" said her father.

Still O Schichi wept. "Oh! oh! oh!" she cried, and swayed herself to and fro.

That night she went to the grove. There was the acolyte, very pale and sorrowful, beneath the trees.

"They will part us," she cried, "O my dear heart's desire. The dear gods are angry with us, and we so young."

"Ah," he said, "I was afraid.... Farewell, dear maid, O little maid, sweet and slender. Remember we are pledged to one another for the space of many existences."

Then the two of them clung together, trembling and weeping, and they bade farewell a thousand times.

The next day they bore O Schichi home to Honjo. She grew languid and listless. White she grew, white as the buckwheat flower. She drooped and she failed. No longer was she numbered with the five beauties of Yedo, nor likened to a cherry- tree in the time of the spring blossoming. All the day long she brooded silently. At night she lay awake in her low bed.

"Oh! oh!" she moaned, "the weary, weary night! Shall I never see him? Must I die of longing? Oh! oh! the weary, weary night...."

Her eyes grew large and burning bright.

"Alas! poor maid," said her father.

"I am afraid ..." said her mother. "She will lose her wits.... She does not weep any more."

At last O Schichi arose and took straw and made it into a bundle; and she put charcoal in the bundle and laid it beneath the gallery of her father's house. Then she set fire to the straw and the charcoal, and the whole burnt merrily. Furthermore the wood of her father's house took light and the house was burnt to the ground.

"I shall see him; I shall see him!" shrieked O Schichi, and fell in a swoon.

Howbeit all the city knew that she had set fire to her father's house. So she was taken before the judge to be tried for her wrongdoing.

"Child," said the judge, "what made you do this thing?"

"I was mad," she said, "I did it for love's sake. I said, 'I will burn the house, we shall have nowhere to lay our heads, then we shall

325

take shelter at the temple; I will see my lover.' Lord, I have not seen him nor heard of him these many, many moons."

"Who is your lover?" said the judge.

Then she told him.

Now as for the law of the city, it was hard and could not be altered. Death was the penalty for the crime of the Yaoya's daughter. Only a child might escape.

"My little maid," the judge said, "are you perhaps twelve years old?"

"Nay, lord," she answered.

"Thirteen, then, or fourteen? The gods send you may be fourteen. You are little and slender."

"Lord," she said, "I am fifteen."

"Alas, my poor maid," said the judge, "you are all too old."

So they made her stand upon the bridge of Nihonbashi. And they told her story aloud; they called it from the house- tops so that all might hear. There she was for all the world to look upon.

Every day for seven days she stood upon the bridge of Nihonbashi, and drooped in the glare of the sun and of men's glances. Her face was white as the flower of the buckwheat. Her eyes were wide and burning bright. She was the most piteous thing under the sky. The tender- hearted wept to see her. They said, "Is this the Yaoya's daughter that was one of the five beauties of Yedo?"

After the seven days were passed they bound O Schichi to a stake, and they piled faggots of wood about her and set the faggots alight. Soon the thick smoke rose.

"It was all for love," she cried with a loud voice. And when she had said this, she died.

"The tale is told," said the ballad- singer. "Youth calls to youth, beauty to beauty, love to love. This is law, and this law was the undoing of the Yaoya's daughter."